SISTERS

ALSO BY DAISY JOHNSON

Fen
Everything Under

DAISY JOHNSON

SISTERS

JONATHAN CAPE
LONDON

1 3 5 7 9 10 8 6 4 2

Jonathan Cape, an imprint of Vintage,
20 Vauxhall Bridge Road,
London SW1V 2SA

Jonathan Cape is part of the Penguin Random House group
of companies whose addresses can be found at
global.penguinrandomhouse.com.

Penguin
Random House
UK

First published by Jonathan Cape in 2020

penguin.co.uk/vintage

A CIP catalogue record for this book is available from the British Library

ISBN 9781787331624 (hardback)
ISBN 9781787331778 (trade paperback)

Typeset in 11.5/16.5 pt Stempel Garamond
by Integra Software Services Pvt. Ltd, Pondicherry

Printed and bound in Great Britain by Clays Ltd, Elcograf S.p.A.

Penguin Random House is committed to a sustainable future for
our business, our readers and our planet. This book is made
from Forest Stewardship Council® certified paper.

MIX
Paper from
responsible sources
FSC
www.fsc.org   FSC® C018179

To my sisters, Polly, Kiran, Sarvat and Jess

To my brothers, Jake and Tom

My sister is a black hole.

My sister is a tornado.

My sister is the end of the line my sister is the locked door my sister is a shot in the dark.

My sister is waiting for me.

My sister is a falling tree.

My sister is a bricked-up window.

My sister is a wishbone my sister is the night train my sister is the last packet of crisps my sister is a long lie-in.

My sister is a forest on fire.

My sister is a sinking ship.

My sister is the last house on the street.

PART ONE

September and July

A house. Slices of it through the hedge, across the fields. Dirty white, windows sunk into the brick. Hand in hand in the back seat, the arrow of light from the sunroof. Two of us, shoulder-to-shoulder, sharing air. A long way to come, up the bone of the country, skimming the Birmingham ring road, past Nottingham, Sheffield and Leeds, breaching the Pennines. This the year we are haunted. What? This the year, as any other, in which we are friendless, necessary only to ourselves. This the year we waited in the rain by the old tennis court for them to arrive. Sounds on the radio: *Higher temperatures are coming from the South ... Police in Whitby.* The shush shush shush of Mum's hands on the wheel. Our thoughts like swallows. Front of the car rising and falling like a bow. There is sea out there somewhere. Pulling the duvet over our heads.

This the year something else is the terror.

*

The road edging away and then dropping from sight, the judder judder judder as we move from tarmac to dirt. Is Mum crying? I don't know. Should we ask? No answer to that and – anyway – the house is there now and no time to go back or try again or do things over. This the year we are houses, lights on in every window, doors that won't quite shut. When one of us speaks we both feel the words moving on our tongues. When one of us eats we both feel the food slipping down our gullets. It would have surprised neither of us to have found, slit open, that we shared organs, that one's lungs breathed for the both, that a single heart beat a doubling, feverish pulse.

July

1

Here we are. Here it is.

This the house we have come to. This the house we have left to find. Beached up on the side of the North York Moors, only just out of the sea. Our lips puckered and wrinkled from licking crisp salt, limbs heavy, wrought with growing pains. The boiling-hot steering wheel, the glare off the road. It has been hours since we left, buried in the back seat. Mum said, getting into the car, Let's make it before night. And then nothing else for a long time. We imagine what she might say: This is your fault, or, We would never have had to leave if you hadn't done what you did. And what she means, of course, is if we hadn't been born. If we hadn't been born at all.

I squeeze my hands together. Not being able to tell yet what the fear is of, only that it is enormous. The house is here. Squatting like a child by the small slate wall, the empty sheep field behind pitted with old excrement, thorn bushes tall as a person. The suck of stale air

7

meeting new as I push the door open. The smell of manure. The hedges overgrown, the grass and weeds forcing their way through the concrete, the front garden narrow and gnarled up with odds and ends, ancient spade heads, plastic bags, shattered plant pots and their almost-living root balls. September up on the uneven garden wall, balancing, teeth clenched in what might or might not be a grin. The windows shuttered with the reflection of her body and of my face beyond, eyeholes like caverns and, beyond that, our mum leaning exhausted against the bonnet.

The white walls of the house are streaked with mud handprints and sag from their wrinkled middles, the top floor sunk down onto the bottom like a hand curved over a fist. Scaffolding heaped against one wall, broken tiles from the roof shattered on the road. I reach for September's arm wondering if I might push my teeth down into the skin to see if I can tell, by the contact, what she is thinking. Sometimes I can. Not with great certainty but with a numb buzz of realisation. Like when Mum turns on the radios in different rooms and the timing is off just a little and you can stand in the corridor in between and hear them echoing; but she whirls away out of reach, cackling like a magpie.

I dig for a tissue in the end of my pocket, blow my nose. The sun is just starting to drop but still it burns on my bare shoulders. There are cough sweets in my pocket, soft with fuzz. I suck one into my cheek.

On the wall of the house there is a sign, covered in grime. I wipe it with my tissue until I can read the words:

THE SETTLE HOUSE. We have never lived in a house with a name before. Never lived in a house that looks the way this one does: rankled, bentoutashape, dirty-allover. September's body spins. I close my eyes five times quickly so that she won't fall and if she does she will land like a cat.

I look back for Mum. She is heaving herself away from the car; her body looks as if it is too much to carry. She has been this way, taciturn or silent, ever since what happened at school. At night we listened to her moving around above us in the Oxford house. She would speak only stray phrases to us, barely meeting our eyes. She is a different person in a recognisable body and I wish she would come back to us. She knocks the garden gate open with her toe.

Help me, she says, as she passes. Ursa said the key was under the frog.

We look for the frog. The ground is loose with insect activity. I dig for a worm and then panic at the feel of it, soft, giving.

Stop mucking around, Mum says and we look bent over in the grass, searching until I find it with my fingers, a stone frog, fat-lipped, button-eyed, almost hidden beneath the undergrowth. Mum tips it with her boot and then groans, no key. Typical, she says. Typical, and then knocks her fists three times against her thighs.

Down the line of the field the May clouds have turned steely and begun gathering and swelling ominously. I point, say, Look.

OK. Quick. Hunt.

We leave the bags in piles and lift the empty pots, kick through the scrub of grass. I find coins in the dirt. Around the side of the house there is a path and a garden with flagstones stacked against the walls, grass torn back to muck, metal rakes abandoned. What might have been a barbecue with a mound of ash inside the split brick structure. There are shells embedded in the side of the house, set into the concrete, and the ground is grainy with sand, loose with sea-smoothed pebbles. I look through one of the windows. Through the glass: the dusky shape of walls, shelves; a pantry perhaps. I spit on my palm and rub. The lighter square of a door frame beyond which there are dim shadows, what might be a sofa or a table, something that could be the first tread of a staircase. Next to me, September presses her face forward, hands curled on the glass, the sweet smell of the perfume we stole from the Boots near our school, the smell of her unbrushed teeth. She goggles her eyes at me, rolls her tongue, pinches my arm. My face looks wrong, the perspective all off, my cheeks longer than they should be, my eyes narrow as coin slots in parking meters.

I look like Mum. Or like her mum she says, our grandmother, in India, where we have never been. September does not look like us. We do not remember our father but she must look like him, smooth-haired, cheeks soft with blonde fuzz, pale-eyed like a snow animal.

The information about him comes drip-drip through the years, rarely wrangled without a fight. He'd met

Mum when she was twenty-three and on holiday in Copenhagen, where he lived at the time. He'd followed her around the city for three days. She told us that he was like that. His English was perfect – he had grown up here – but he liked to speak to her in Danish, enjoyed the fact that she could not understand. He was like that too. He had died. How had he died? we asked for four years before she caved. He had drowned in the swimming pool of a hotel in Devon. They had not been together when he died and the three of us, September barely five, me a little younger, had been living somewhere else. It had taken nearly a year for his sister to ring and tell her he was dead. We learned not to ask about him. We do not have the words to describe him. We did not know him. September once said to Mum that he was a howlingbanderlootinggrifter and she had laughed and said it was true but had then gone quiet for a few hours, got the look we had come to recognise. Every three or four Christmases his sister Ursa comes to visit and September and I sometimes try and wring information out of her but she never caves. Ursa drives a convertible car, never comes for more than a day, stays in a hotel rather than at ours. Her hair is short and blonde so that, coming upon her from behind and unawares, we would at times be convinced that she was him; long-lost father, the reason for our mother's sadness and our existence. The house on the moors belongs to her though she rents it out, does not live here, fills it with people like us who do not know where else to go.

Down the side of the house, the wind picking up a bit now, we find another window, not large but loose-looking, opening inwards when we press on it.

At the front of the house Mum has a rock out of a nearby field and is about to throw it through the pane of glass beside the door. I lift my hands to cover my ears. The blood goes boom boom boom and the alarm grows in my bone marrow and swans up my throat.

There's an open window, September yells. I think we can fit inside. Mum turns her stony face towards us, mouth drawn down and carved into the skin.

The room the window leads into is a pantry. We are holding hands by the time we get inside. Beneath the window there is a dirty tiled floor, chipped where it meets the damp wall. Wooden shelves. Some cans of soup and beans, a couple of packets of off-coloured spaghetti. There is a smell, almost sweet with an undertone that I cannot quite identify. The ceiling is low and the bare bulb bumps off the top of my head.

September is humming the way she does when she is excited and wants me to know it. Her hums can mean all sorts of things. Hello, where are you/ Come here/ Stop that/ I'm annoyed with you. I realise that I am afraid of the house and of Mum being angry and of September being annoyed. We have been here before, only once, but I do not remember it well.

What is that? I say.

What?

That smell.

I don't know. A dead mouse?

Don't say that.

Through the door of the pantry we can see into the corridor beyond; to the left is the front entrance and, beside it, another closed door leading, perhaps, to a bathroom. Ahead are the stairs and to the right another door and in front of us, opening out, a sitting room. The layout of the house feels wrong, unintuitive, the pantry opening directly onto the sitting room the way it does. It smells like food left out too long. They go out into the sitting room. In the corner of the room there is a hunched shape, formless, folds of material. I squeeze September's hand. It is impossible that we are here and it is impossible to stay. There is a lamp on the table nearest us that I lunge for. Something is knocked from the table and falls. My insides are filled with bees. The light comes on, emitting a high-pitched whine.

There's nothing there, September says. Don't worry, July-bug.

She goes around turning on switches. Everything is a little too bright, as if the bulbs are not quite right for their fixtures. There is the smell of burning and, when I look into one of the deep-bowled lamps, I see the mulch of web, the dead flies in the base. There are mangy blankets on the sofa and the armchair, a coffee table with a couple of mugs on it, a pile of newspapers below. There is a wood-burning stove underneath a wooden mantle with a dirty rug in front. A small window lets in a little light. The ceiling is low and beamed. If we were any taller we would have to bend. Behind the stairs there are empty bookcases. The thing I'd knocked from the table is on the floor, half under the sofa. When I pick it up there is dirt on my hands. The glass is broken jaggedly. September puts her arms around my middle and her chin on my shoulder.

Don't worry, look, it's an ant farm.

I turn it the other way up. She's right. Two panes of glass welded into a narrow box and filled with dirt. There are tunnels, excavations, runnels set through the earth, falling in on themselves as we move it.

I broke it, I say and feel – thick, cloying, unavoidable – what it would be like to live in the dirt and force your way mouthily through.

We can fix it, she says. There will be tape somewhere. We'll find some ants to put inside.

There is a rapping at the door, Mum reminding us. I go to let her in. Her face looks so tired, as if she hasn't slept in a week. It had been a long winter, a bad Christmas already flavoured with what would come, a creeping spring. There had been the fight at school in March, the sodden surface of the abandoned tennis courts, the mud on our bare feet and my hands looking as if they belonged to someone else. We'd stayed in Oxford for two months after what had happened and now it's May, the storms given way to heat. I want to touch Mum's face, have her hold me the way she used to do when we would all pile into the double bed. Except she is already pushing past, jaw rigid, the bags dropping from her hands to the floor. I have felt tired too, since we left school; some days it is as if I am carrying a second body draped over my shoulders. I want to tell her this, have her say she is the same or that she can help me feel better.

We watch her going up the stairs. September whistles between her teeth and says her name – the way she does when she wants to annoy her – quietly, Sheela, and for a moment it looks like she hesitates and might come back but then she is forging forward, boots on the wooden steps. She's got her duvet under one arm, her work folder under the other. We stand listening to her until there is the sound of a door closing. She has been sad before but it was not the same as this. This is worse.

She's so angry, I say. I can feel September's rising annoyance.

She won't be angry forever, she says.

She might be.

Not at you, September says and pulls my plait, makes my eyes water.

The door furthest from the front of the house leads into a small galley kitchen. There are caked baking trays in the sink, an empty bread bag on the side, more mugs. There is a tiny window. I grapple awkwardly up onto the counter, pull at the catch except it won't open, has, I see, been painted shut, nails forced into the soft wood for good measure. I get down. There are yellow notes stuck to the fridge – I recognise Ursa's handwriting from the birthday cards – the A and J from a set of magnetic letters. It feels intrusive to read the notes but I do, leaning forward, looking for some kind of secret language or information to show September. But there are only details about bin days, a door at the back that sticks, a list of what not to put in the fire. The kitchen around me is so dirty it makes me itch. I let the tap run until it comes cold and then scrub my hands but even the water feels coated, soft with slime. From the doorway September whistles for me, a few notes, drawing me back together.

All right, July-bug?

Yes.

Next to the pantry there is a bathroom with a bathtub and a toilet. September tugs at the halogen. There are signs of someone having been here and not long ago: a sliver of soap on the scummy sink, a couple of shampoo bottles dropped into the bath, a smudge of what might be make-up on the floor.

Whose stuff is this? I say, nudging the soap with my thumbnail and then feeling sick.

Don't know. One of Ursa's renters. I heard Mum on the phone with her, I think she turfed them out so we could stay.

How long are we going to be here?

Why are you asking me? September huffs and then, I don't know why Mum would want us to come.

Dead skin, I say, running my finger along the sink and September glares at me and marches through the door.

My teeth feel furry with the long journey, the cheese and onion sandwiches we'd bought from a service station somewhere. I remember, suddenly, that we have left behind our toothbrushes, propped up on the sink in the old house, the house we will not be going back to. I go into the sitting room to tell September but she is upstairs; I can hear her moving around. Some of the dirt shifts in the ant farm, as if something had just moved through it.

Warm air comes beneath the front door and down the chimney. I want to hear my voice against the white walls. The room has the feeling of having been busy moments before. I say September's name as quietly as I can but even that is too loud. I can feel all the rooms behind me. It is impossible to face every part of the house at once; I look in the kitchen and the pantry but they are empty, filled only with the murmur of the low lights. I go up the stairs fast, two at a time. Something behind me, something on my heels. Except, at the top looking back, there is nothing there.

The narrow hallway has three rooms leading off it. The nearest is a bedroom with a bunk bed wedged into one corner, no other furniture. The bunk beds had not been here before, we had slept – I think – on mattresses on the floor. There are things I remember and things that are not the same. I can't see September and then she sits up on the top bunk and laughs at me. My blood presses at my throat.

Where did you go? My voice is high, dog-whistle-like. Often – since we were young – I wait for her to abandon me, to go her own way.

I went here, she says. I wanted to see where we were sleeping. Look. She is holding a pair of battered binoculars.

What are they?

You know what they are.

I remember the photo we'd found of Dad once, crushed into the glove compartment of Ursa's fancy car; he looked maybe ten and the binoculars were around his neck. He nearly broke my arm over those, Ursa said when she caught us, tugging the photo from September's grip.

There are marks from old posters on the walls and a clock over the door. The bunk bed is narrow like a bench. September shimmies down the ladder and waves her arms: ta-da.

Sometimes I think I can remember the days when we were so small we slept in one cot, four hands twisting above our heads, seeing the world from exactly the same vantage point. I couldn't talk then but I think, still, we must have understood one another. I wish and wish for it to be that way now. Or when we were a little older and she'd heave herself over the bars of the crib and drop down, yell at me to do the same until Mum came in and put her back or took us into her bed, all of our arms tangled then, Mum's chest under our cheeks, September's eyes so close to mine that I could see each teary eyelash. I say to September: Do you wish it were that way? Do you wish it was still like that? And she says, I don't know what you're talking about, July.

We crouch outside Mum's closed door but there is nothing to hear. This has happened before, listening through this door. She is asleep, maybe. We open the third door off the corridor. It is an airing cupboard. There is a great bellied water tank and a complicated array of controls for heat and hot water. There are mouse traps on the floor but nothing caught in them. We stand considering the buttons. We can hear the insides of the tank churning. The rain is coming down tinnily on the roof. Through the palm of September's hand I think I could probably hear the slow motion of her thoughts if I listened well enough, the chuckle of words. I remember those last few weeks at school. It had rained often, flooding the gutters, sheeting down the windows. There had been a dead badger we'd seen from the car on the way in. The other girls' faces. There is only one reason we have left the house in Oxford and come here, and though it had been September's idea to get those girls to the old tennis court, to teach them a lesson, to scare them just a bit, September is not the reason we're at the Settle House. There is only one person at fault for that.

September is jabbing at the buttons on the boiler at random. She still has the binoculars around her neck and they move as she does. From behind the wall there is a bovine groan.

I don't think that was right.

The floor rattles a little under our feet.

Maybe not, September says. Let's go downstairs, I'm hungry.

We go to raid the fridge but there is nothing to be raided. The tins in the small room by the door are years out of date, bent as if someone has battered them.

Let's do something else, she says.

The rain comes sideways against the windows. We flop on our bellies on the sitting-room floor and September talks about what colours we will paint our walls, the posters we will put up. I am only half listening. The room feels the way it did before, as if there is activity happening just out of view. September holds the binoculars to her face and swivels them.

I lean into the pantry and fumble for the light switch. The bulb is shifting in the small room, illuminating one wall and then the other, throwing the shelves into relief and then into shadow. I peer at the tins, not wanting to move further into the room, and the bulb makes a click-click sound and then blows, dropping the room back into darkness.

September finds a chicken pie in the kitchen freezer and we decide to try and cook it. While we wait we watch old downloads of January Hargrave interviews on our laptop. I try to listen at the same time to the sound of Mum coming down to forgive us. To forgive us for everything.

I don't think we should stay tomorrow if the Internet isn't up, September says.

We leave the pie in for too long. I hold it over the bin while September tries to scrape the burn off the top.

I grilled it.

Never mind.

Except it is raw inside when we cut it open. Pink flecks of chicken which I spit into September's open hand. She doesn't even taste it. We fork the whole thing into the bin.

I don't want to go into the pantry again but September sighs at me and wades into the dark, comes out with her arms filled with dented tins. There is one of peaches which is only a year out of date. September hacks at it with a knife and then gives it to me to suck the juice from the gap. I am suddenly so hungry I feel dizzy. I take the knife from her and gouge at the opening, widening it until I can get my fingers in, jabbing out peaches, swallowing them without chewing.

Do you want any?

Not hungry any more, she says.

We sit on the floor rather than the sofa. There is quiet for a while. The peach syrup is gritty. September puts on a Darcey Lewis album on her phone, and we know all the words.

She sits up straighter, says, I was born here.

What do you mean?

She doesn't answer. There is a creep of cold down the chimney, a finger. We can hear the boiler in the walls. I get up on my knees.

What do you mean you were born here?

I mean. I was born here. I overheard Mum on the phone the other night talking to that bookseller friend. Mum said: It's probably the same bed, actually.

I thought we were both born in Oxford.

So did I. But only you were. I was born in this house.

It had, I realise, meant something that we had been born in the same place. Ten months apart, the same hospital, the same bed perhaps; one chasing the other out. September and then – soon enough we might as well have come together – me.

Mum doesn't like this house, she says.

Why do you think that?

21

I just know. She didn't like it when we were all here before. You remember that summer we were here? She didn't like it then and she doesn't like it now.

You don't know that.

September bares her teeth. I do.

How?

I just do. From things Mum said.

What else did she say?

That there was nowhere else to go. She came here with him and Ursa when I was inside her. And later, when she was sad, September says. She opens her arms out to take in the low-ceilinged sitting room, the ant farm, the stained coffee table, the mouth of the kitchen door. Dad was born here and I was too. I remember.

I look at her to see if she is lying. I know that sometimes she lies to me for fun or to see if I can catch her out and sometimes she lies because she can and I'm not sure why. I put the peach tin in the bin. The evening sinks away.

Later, half asleep – the sound of September whispering in my ear, the sound of Mum crying in the room at the end of the hallway. Half asleep – the pressure of her fingers on the sides of my face.

2

Sleep is heavy, without corners, dreamless. I wake to the light through the curtains, roll over, doze once more. I keep almost making it out, struggling, falling back under. My throat is dry like sand. I swallow and swallow. Peel myself up. The clock over the door frame: twelve o'clock. Half the day already gone. My chest is sore and when I peer down there are red marks around my breastbone. September is not in the top bunk. I go down into the kitchen and stand with my face underneath the tap drinking down great gulps and then stand still listening for movement.

September? No answer.

I go into the sitting room. There are the leftovers from our night, the pillows pulled onto the floor, our water glasses, the laptop balanced on the arm of the sofa.

September was my sleep shadow. We were ten or eleven. I would be woken by the light from the fridge which I had opened in my dream or the cold from the window

I had jimmied wide and she would be behind me, hands on my shoulders, leading me back to bed. For a year it was bad. The seam between sleep and waking grew thin. I would come out of a dream about something hanging from the ceiling and it would still be there, about to drop. The days flooded with dream logic. I would think that I had lost something and spend hours looking half-heartedly for an object I had never even owned. And always September would be there, hushing me as I woke already screaming, searching with me for the mysterious lost item. I became afraid. I grew convinced that sleep was a land of its own and if I opened the door and went into it nothing good would ever happen again. Often the supposed consequences would be to do with September. If I went to sleep September would leave. If I went to sleep September would die from electrocution or drowning or fire or being buried alive. We spent a lot of time on the Internet trying to work me out of my fears. The fear of being buried alive is called taphephobia; the fear of water is aquaphobia; the fear of electric shock is called hormephobia. I got good at sleeping for as little time as possible. Dreams were tangles, dreams were marshes, dreams were the coffin our father was buried in. By the end of the year the fear had begun to run itself out and I could sleep again. We built routines to help: soak your feet in hot water when you wake up to wash away the dreams, brush your hair before you go to bed.

The last time we were in this house was the year I did not sleep. We came for a season. Mum was sick, took three pills a day, slept a lot. The year before

September had insisted we merge our birthdays into one day and so it didn't matter, really, how old we were. We went to the beach and Mum slept on a blanket and we made sandcastles, buried one another up to the neck. Sometimes Mum would wade into the water and I'd hold on to her front and September on to her back and we'd ride the waves, swallowing foam, yelling at the cold. Sometimes we would drive to the nearest town and the three of us would share fish and chips, the sting of vinegar, the crust of salt. At the house Mum would rub lemon juice into September's hair so that it glowed whiter than ever.

We played games in the dark. Our eyes grew accustomed to the lack of light and we could move around the house without bumping into anything; that was the first game. The second game was called September Says and was a game we had stolen and changed. September was in charge and I was the puppet and had to do whatever she said. If she said September says stand on your head or September says write your name on the wall in permanent marker then I had to do it. If she said stand on your head or write your name on the wall in permanent marker then I wasn't allowed to do it and if I accidentally did then I would lose a life. Most games I had five lives and after I'd lost all of them then something would happen, although every game the thing that happened would be different and it would always depend on how September was feeling that day. It was not really about the lives or about winning or losing, it was about playing the game.

We had played September Says almost constantly when we were in the Settle House that last time. In the daylight the things I had to do were easy: September says do a roly-poly. September says cross your eyes. Turn around on the spot, you lose a life. As the day drained away the tasks would get harder: September says cut off your fingernails and put them in the milk. Cut off all your hair. September says lie down under the bed for an hour. Run into the road. September says put all your clothes in the bin and stand in front of the window. Put this needle through your finger.

It was a good game. We played it the entire time we were at the house but after we left it didn't feel right and we stopped.

Some days Mum was better and some days she was worse. We both got used to seeing the signs. September used to say that she wished Mum wasn't there so it could just be us but I liked it when she was around, when it was the three of us. I liked it at the Settle House when we went for walks along the cliffs all together and Mum would tell us the names of the plants we could see or the plots for the story she was thinking of writing. September liked it best when it was just the two of us but I liked it when we were three, hand in hand, Mum in the middle, swaying our arms.

When Mum was having a bad day we kept out of her way; sometimes she wandered around the house as if looking for something but one evening we were playing and heard her as she went downstairs, out the front door. We watched from the window as she got into the car and drove off. It had happened before and so we knew she would be back.

September says pretend to be a house, September said.

I wasn't sure what to do but I stretched out my arms and my legs and curled myself round to try and make walls and cupped my hands to make little porthole windows and I swung my arm to show that the door was opening and closing. I laughed.

September says don't laugh, September said. She crawled onto my lap and tugged my arms around her like the walls of the house were closing around her body and we stayed that way for a long time even though I got pins and needles. At some point the house grew legs and hid from her and she chased it.

It got dark and we looked for the car out of the window, watching for headlights across the hill.

There? I said.

No, she said.

Then, a moment later: There?

No, wait, no not there either.

We pretended to be trees growing through the floors of the house, birds in the trees, mice in the walls.

Listen, September said later and we ran to the window and she was right, there were headlights coming, four eyes, throwing different parts of the road and the fields into view. We watched them coming and then got onto the mattress in our room, pulled the duvet over our heads, held our breath. There had been four headlights and then there were four feet, on the stairs and pausing outside our door and then going on towards Mum's bedroom. We rolled onto the floor, crawled out into the corridor.

Outside her door we listened for a long time, shushing one another, flat on our fronts. The noises were so strange, like listening to animals we did not know existed. I could feel the cold floor under me, my knee was itching. My eyelids flickered between sleeping and waking but when I looked at September she was unblinking, barely breathing. How could it be that one moment you knew nothing and the next you knew everything? The house took the noise and grew it louder, tunnelled it towards us. I thought I could make out Mum's voice but I couldn't be certain; it could have been another woman, one we did not know. There was a man's voice too.

A cough rose in my throat and spilled over, September grabbed my hand and we got up and ran back to our bedroom and got into bed and lay there not moving.

The next day September said that everything felt different and I couldn't decide if she was right or not. She said it was not a small change but a heavy difference.

Out of the tiny sitting-room window the sky is aged, the ribbon of potholed road winding away, the hill or mountain half seen above the rest. I think that perhaps I can hear the sea, hope that we will go there. My feet are bare and the floor so cold it feels like stone. I wish we were in Oxford with the endless sound of Mum working in the study above our heads and September standing by the open door of the bedroom and saying that it is time to get up and see the eclipse.

Mum must have been down in the night because there is the beginning of unpacking: the TV in the far corner, a selection of books stacked against the wall. She must have been shopping too because there is food in the pantry, the sort of thing September would call apocalypse fare: more tins of fruit and of beans, long-life milk. The house doesn't feel busy the way it had done the night before. It feels empty. As if I've been abandoned while I slept. On the kitchen counter there are new light bulbs. I take one out of the packet and hold it.

September? The house groans around me, releasing air. I look into the pantry. I think of telling September that I'd changed the bulb alone and reach up to unscrew it. I cup it in my hands but do not turn it. I put the new light bulb on one of the shelves, pushing it back from the side and go to check I've turned off the light switch. There is a noise from the bathroom, momentarily distracting me, and then the shatter of breaking glass behind me in the pantry. There is just enough light from the sitting room to see the new bulb in pieces on the floor, the glass spread out towards my feet. I close the pantry and go towards the bathroom, push the door open. There is a bite of almost fear in my temples. September is in the tub, slick-headed, blowing out a stream of soapy water from her mouth.

Where were you? I say. I can hear the tinge of desperation in my voice. I was calling you. I broke a bulb.

29

She slaps her hands up and down on the surface, splashing the floor. You slept for a year.

Not a year. Can I come in?

I'm done, she says and raises her big toe with the chain of the plug wrapped around it. The water gurgles away. Shall we make a weird feast and watch something? She hoists herself out.

I feel bereft at her having had a bath without me. At home we had them together often, the laptop propped up on the chair so we could watch David Attenborough or listen to ancient episodes of *Desert Island Discs*. September likes her baths boiling hot, likes eating cold things in them: raspberry-ripple ice creams, Magnums which often slip from their sticks. I know September's body better than I know my own. Often – looking down at myself – there is a great mass of confusion and in the mirror there is a shock at seeing my own face looking back rather than hers. She has a coiled-snake birthmark on the arch of her left foot, her skin goes red quickly under the sun, there is a long black hair on her collarbone that I want badly to pluck out but that she says she is growing forever. I will always think that September's body makes more sense than my own. I hand her a towel. She looks larger than she did in Oxford, as if she is taking up more space. I prod her on the hip. Why did you have one without me?

I don't know. I wanted to, I guess.

*

September clears up the broken bulb with a dustpan and brush and we put in a new one and then try on dresses out of the dressing-up box we get from the car. We paint big lipstick smiles around the outsides of our mouths and then leave kisses on the windows. We are hoarders; there are holes in the elbows of some of the dresses, fraying beneath the armpits, food stains on the hem. The favourite pair of shoes that we take turns wearing has worn through almost to the ground. I settle on a dress with a lace panel and thin silken sleeves and watch while September rummages through the box.

Don't stand there watching me, she says.

What shall I do?

Go look in the pantry.

There are chickpeas and chopped tomatoes and bags of rice but I do not want to cook. The bulb burns brighter than it should for five minutes and then blows again. I hold my breath in the dark, trying not to be afraid. There are footsteps on the stairs and I go out into the sitting room, planning to tell September about the bulb and the food. It is Mum. Her hair is dirty, tied up on top of her head. She is wearing a lot of clothes although the heating is pumping. Her pyjamas are stained and she has a mug and a plate in her hands. She came down in the night to eat so she didn't have to see us. That is what happened. She stops on the stairs and looks at me and then turns her head, looking for September, who has stopped looking in the box and is on the sofa, does not even glance away from the telly.

31

I need to wash these up, Mum says after a moment. Will you come to the kitchen with me?

The kitchen is too small for all three of us. September pulls herself up onto the counter and glowers. Mum pushes the plug into the sink and runs the tap. Looking at her I remember the night of the book launch. She had worn a gold dress, red shoes with velvet ribbon that laced up her calves. Her cheeks had been flushed with wine, her arms around both our shoulders. At midnight she had taken off her shoes in the pub and stood barefoot talking to someone from the bookshop. September had put her face very close to my ear and said, She looks like a goddess. We had loved her then, willingly, unendingly, in a way that I think we do not often do. Mostly she is just there. Mostly she is just a mother to us and she is in rooms the way chairs and tables are.

The house burbles around us. The water chokes out of the tap. She doesn't catch our eyes. She washes and then passes things to me and I dry them and then give them to September to put in the cupboard. I want to tell Mum how we're sorry, really sorry, about what happened at the school and that maybe we could go to the beach together or have dinner. I want September to say it too and when I look at her she shrugs and says, Mum –

I just need some time, Mum says. I feel the words breaking through the quiet. I feel them against my arms and face. She puts the dishcloth down and turns towards us. I will always love you, she says. And if you need me you come get me. But I need some time. OK?

We nod and then she is gone.

I drink the juice out of another peach tin and September makes me pasta and butter, which I eat sitting on the counter. September says she doesn't want any, but I am still so hungry.

Is there anything else?

She tuts but hacks open another tin, of pears this time, which I eat all of. My skeleton feels close to the skin, rubbing painfully at the joints, my cheekbones grating.

We watch an episode of *33* we must have seen twenty times with the sound on mute so that the characters' mouths open and close but their voices are stolen away. It is our favourite series. An early January Hargrave – our favourite director – creation in which two women – one a pathologist and one a librarian – known only by their surnames, Hadley and Bell, track strange goings-on in remote locations, date unsuitable people and, a few times a season, die and then come back again. When we are bored we watch nature programmes. We like the lizards, the reptiles, the snakes that move across the sand with their heads and stomachs raised up. We like the fleshy massacre scenes, herds of lions taking down gazelles or leopards in trees with their prey slung over the branches. We like Attenborough's calm voice, as if he controls everything that happens, no animal moving without his say-so. The animals run and stop and swim and burrow and feast and die. We stay still on the sofa, breathe and digest and tingle and grow warm and then cold.

I'm bored, September says, pinching my arm, the skin turning momentarily white.

Only boring people are bored, I say, parroting Mum, and September pinches harder and then points over my shoulder.

Let's fill that.

I look where she is pointing. The ant farm is on the table where we left it.

It's got holes in it.

So? We'll find some tape. Come on. You look in the kitchen.

I open and close drawers, pretending to search. I imagine the ant farm spilling out in the night and waking to find the sheets crusty with them. There is gaffer tape on top of the fridge with a pile of old mail. I stand holding it until September comes in and takes it off me.

Don't you want to?

Yes.

It'll be fun. They make their own house. Did you know a crushed ant leaves a pheromone mark that makes other ants in the vicinity go into attack mode?

She is squatting on the floor with the ant farm between her knees. She patches it and then trims the tape back so we can see inside. My skin itches and I dig my fingers into my hair to stop from scratching. September props the ant farm up on the table and winds a scarf around me, jams my arms into the sleeves of Mum's coat, pushes my feet into some boots we find by the door. The clouds have not given up their rain and it is warm, windless. There is the smell of sea salt. We crouch outside the door and explore, lifting leaves and pushing muck aside. I find a beetle and a thin crust of spiderweb. September ferrets near the wall, hopping forward without rising. She says the ground looks ant-disturbed but we do not find any. I know she is annoyed by the way she knocks her tongue around her mouth and whistles at me to keep looking. I find a few more rusty coins, my fingers slick with dirt, the mulch of dead leaves. I want to go inside, hold my hands under the tap; but I cannot go until she does. We search for what feels like a long time. September finds the beetle I saw earlier and, grunting, scoops it up and deposits it in the farm. We watch it rushing around, knocking into the glass.

It's not an ant. Do beetles even dig? I say, but she only pinches the skin on my arms again and kicks off her boots. When she is angry with me I don't know what to do with myself.

I feel dizzy and have to sit down. There are whole sentences in my head but when I try and say them the words choke themselves and my head jerks and not a single sound comes out. September puts her hot hand on my forehead and I close my eyes and when I open them she has moved away although the feeling of her hand lingers, too warm, against my skin.

September says: Do you remember the eclipse?

We'd got up early to see it. Mum had made us break-fast – scrambled eggs, bread from the corner shop – and then gone to work in the attic. We were about eleven. The night before we'd made a box with a hole in it, carefully measured. I had sliced myself on the box cutter and stood frozen in horror until September did the same, laughed, showed me the drip of red on the floor.

That was the day I had promised her everything a person could promise.

We took the box out onto the pavement. There were people going to work. No one else seemed even to notice what was happening. There was a blindness to the world we could not believe. We stood on the stoop and watched the dark circle cover the light. It had been thrilling and wonderful and for the next week I had dreamed of the eclipse blotting out my eyes, seeping into my blood.

It burned, September says and I know she means the moment when we dared each other, barely breathing, and moved the box away, stared upwards. A whole day with the imprint of that bolt at the corners of our eyes and me thinking that it was the only time we would see something so exactly the same. Wishing it could always be that way.

A man turns up to sort out the Internet. He has falling down trousers and doesn't seem to like us much, even when we make him a cup of tea with the long-life milk from the pantry. We hover around the phone line as he toils.

How does it work? September says.

How does what work? He has skinny haunches like a goat and a receding hairline. I think that he looks like

36

a January Hargrave character and September, catching the thought, snorts through her nose. We seem to be able to hear one another more here. I wonder if it is being in this place, where our father and then September were both born, where the sound of the rooms seems so different from anywhere we have lived before. The man looks at us out of the corner of his eye, flips the tool he's using upside down.

The Internet, I say and September laughs behind her cupped hands.

How does the Internet work? He looks at us as if we're mad.

Yes.

I suppose, he says, it sends radio frequencies between devices. Is that good enough?

I don't think that's true, September says. But I say: Yes.

He turns to us with his hands on his bony hips. Well, which is it? Yes or no.

Yes, I say, mostly.

There is an issue with the router. He goes outside and speaks to someone on the phone, head lowered against the sun, which has dropped. We peer at him out of the window and then rummage through his bag, pulling out wires and chargers, tapping at the screen of the tablet buried at the bottom, sniffing the cigarette packet and Thermos of coffee. Halfway through looking I get so nervous my hands won't move and September looks for both of us, digging, shoving things around, clicking her tongue up and down in her mouth. We hear him outside, the sound of his feet on the uneven ground. She turns and looks up at me and then puts something in her pocket and hustles me into the kitchen where we stand together at the open fridge, looking in. He eyes us.

Do you want beans? September says. There isn't any cheese but there are beans in the pantry.

Nope, he says and bends to look in the bag.

We watch him out of the corner of our eyes, moving our mouths as if whispering to one another, opening and closing the fridge. I catch him watching us warily and look away while September grits her teeth in a white grin. He mostly ignores us and we get bored and bundle onto the sofa and watch the Attenborough episode on television where the monkey swims through the forest, cautious eyes above the waterline. He must not have even needed the thing that she took. I am relieved. At one point September goes into the bathroom and closes the door, runs the tap so I know she is pretending to use the toilet. The man is bent over the bag again, trousers sagging.

Did you take something from here? he says.

I bite my tongue.

Did you hear me? he says. Did you take a cable from here?

I shake my head.

It was here when I looked before. Come on, he says, standing now. No mucking around. You hear? Where did you put it? In the fridge. Good one. Come on then.

He goes to the kitchen and stares into the fridge. September opens the bathroom door. We didn't take it, she says loudly, covering the man's grumbled complaints from the kitchen. We didn't bloody take it.

Good one, he says, shoving his hands into the pockets of his trousers and rounding his chin at us. That's a good one. Come on. Out with it. You want Internet or not?

You want Internet or not, September says. Her body braced, her fingers curled to claws, her mouth slit to nastiness.

Enough of this, he says.

Enough of this, September says.

He blinks at me, pleadingly. I say nothing. He doesn't understand. What does he want me to say?

I'll finish in ten minutes if you let me. Be out of your hair.

Out of your hair, September says.

Christ.

Christ.

I can't go until I'm done, he says and spreads his hands out in front of him.

I'm done, September says. Her grin is vast. Nausea clenches around my sides. The man doesn't say anything else. He opens and closes his hands, seems about to speak and then doesn't. The silence is longer than comfortable. September goes back into the bathroom. I shrug my shoulders, try to apologise without letting September see that I am doing so. He goes outside and there is the sound of him opening the door of his van. He is looking, I think, for another cable.

In the bathroom September is sitting in the empty tub, arms hanging over the sides, head tipped back. Her eyes are open and pale, the whites swallowing the pupils.

Why did you do that? I say.

Why not? she says.

There is the sound of the man coming back in and moving around the room. I get into the empty bath with September. We listen to the noises of the house and of the man setting up the Internet. At times September shifts or sits up and looks around and I think that she might be about to go back and bait him again, force him into a corner the way she had done before. But she stays in the bath, flicking the chain with the plug on back and forth, occasionally smiling at me as if we are sharing a joke, and after a while – not long – there is the noise of the van driving away up the road.

I didn't like him, September says. Don't make a big deal out of it. She jumps out of the bath and goes into the sitting room, singing.

There is Wi-Fi, finally, and – despite everything that happened – September lets out a crow of relief. She opens five tabs at the same time and we listen to a Darcey Lewis album and cruise through a Google map of the area, trying to remember, last time we were here, how far away the beach was. There is a route across the field and down a slope, and then there is the sea.

Do you think we'll go to school here? I say. We are lying head-to-head on the carpet picking bits out of the shag. September's head is bony like a dinosaur's and her hair smells of dirt and smoke. We have left behind what happened with the Internet man, we will not talk about it again because September does not want to.

I don't think so.

Won't we get in trouble?

With who?

I don't know what to say to that. We watch enough television that my eyes sting and a headache starts. September massages my scalp a little more forcefully than is comfortable. We use the laptop at the same time, and it makes the headache worse. We have profiles on a couple of websites, photos taken from search engines. Often, we pretend to be women we are not and message with older men or they message us; we use our hands to cover our mouths so Mum can't hear our laughing at the language they use, the photos they send. At the end of the day we reveal ourselves like a magic trick. September says we are jailbait or she says that we are undercover police. The men will delete their accounts or they will send awful messages and September likes it best when they do that. She writes replies that are just as awful and are sometimes worse. She always takes it too far and I have to pretend to be looking when really I'm thinking about other things. We like the Reddit threads about TV shows or films, discussions on character or plot. We like Wikipedia, the stores of endless knowledge, the over-swelling of fact, the mistakes and lies buried within the truth. Last summer we grew obsessed by computer viruses, the wriggling, pliable creatures that swarmed or worked their way in gently, went unnoticed for months, years. There are rumours of a new January Hargrave film in the deeper echelons and we read these again, comment on a couple begging for more information.

Shall we go outside?

It's nice to be in all day, September says and stretches out until the bones in her wrists click. It's not like her to say such a thing. In Oxford she was the restless one, wanting always to go down to the river to swim or catch the bus out to the countryside.

It's different here, September says. Something is different. She makes a sucking noise with her head close to my face, and then, into my ear: Do you remember?

What?

I think of the tennis courts murky with the rain which had been coming all day, falling loudly onto the skylights during biology and the leaking roof of the sports hall and the dead badger and the hood of her raincoat moving through the muddy forest ahead of me.

In the Settle House my face feels hot, the neck of my dress too high for comfort. I raise my head off the floor. In the far corner of the room a miniature of the house is floating, open like one of those perfectly created doll's houses. The rooms are like organs, trembling a little under the flow of blood. In one of the bedrooms a tiny version of Mum is sat working at the drawing board, a cup of coffee at her elbow. The bunk bed is unmade, with the clothes we'd tried on thrown over. There is someone in the bottom bunk, someone with hair like mine. Downstairs the bath is full, nearly overflowing, brown with mud.

42

September is in the kitchen, standing by the open fridge with the light on her face and September is also in the bathroom and September is also on the sofa, laptop balanced on her tiny lap, eyes moving across the screen and September is also crouched on the roof, clinging on.

She has her mouth close to my ear and is saying something, her breath inside my head.

What?

Nothing. Where were you? September says.

When I blink there is an after-image of the house behind my eyelids, like an imprint of the eclipse. What time is it?

I don't know. Four o'clock.

We check the flashing clock on the cooker. It's ten to eight. It is going dark outside the window and we had not noticed. The day feels sucked away; the hours swallowed. I am hungry again but, looking in the pantry, there is nothing I feel like eating. The house is boiling and when I put my hand against the radiator it leaves a scorched mark. We stomp upstairs to check the boiler and find the heating turned up high.

Do you think it's this one? September says but, though she presses every button she can and turns all the dials, nothing seems to change. What shall we do now?

I shake my head, which is pounding in time to the heat throbbing through the walls. I wish we could knock on Mum's door, lure her out, but I won't suggest it, not if September won't.

She wouldn't even if we asked, September says. She doesn't want to be with us right now.

3

There had been trouble back in Oxford before. I knew that sometimes I forgot where I was or sang out loud, knew that the other girls – and some of the boys – saw me doing those things and counted them as weakness. A few times they took my bag on the bus and stole things from it or knocked over my water glass at lunch. I'd seen my name in the stalls in the toilets: *July sucks it. July's got no life.* Always it died down or they found a more interesting target or September made it clear that she wouldn't stand for it. I don't know how it made me feel. Often, at school or at the kitchen table with Mum, I felt as if I moved a little outside of my body, could not quite touch or see anything entirely. It was only when September was around that colour returned and I could experience pain or smell the lunch cooking in the school kitchens. She tethered me. Not to the world but to herself.

I liked to watch them. These other people, so unlike us. The girls especially. The way they moved. They were assertive but not too assertive, bold but not too bold, clever but not too clever. They were playing a game we did not know how to play.

I had ignored them for a long time but in the new year something had changed and by March it had got worse. Perhaps it was the weather – which was bad – or the fact that there were exams coming up, or perhaps it was something I did or it was nothing at all. On the bus I could hear their quick-fire voices from the back row, the way they used my name, September stiffening against me. In class they moved pack-like, their shoulders buffeting me from side to side. Their names were Kirsty and Jennifer and Lily and they were mean. They had always been mean but there was something that week that ramped them up, drove them on.

There was a group of boys who flitted around them, followed them in the corridor or loitered by their lockers. One of them – Ryan Driver – had long eyelashes and bashful freckles and I always felt great disappointment in the way that he laughed when Lily said anything.

He's an idiot, September said and wouldn't speak on the subject. But I liked him. That was it. I liked him. I felt it in my muscles and my skin. I lost words around him. I liked the way he looked and spoke, the shape and sound of him.

The three girls carved penises and boobs into the metal of my locker. They hissed and catcalled my name in the corridors. They stole all of my gym clothes from my locker and scattered them around the school.

Never mind, I said, gathering them up.

I do mind, September grunted and sometimes she retaliated in small ways; barging past them through doors, staring at them across the classroom.

At night in our bedroom we crushed coffee beans with our fists and tore strips off the bottoms of our dresses, wound them around our bare arms, wet our hair and fingers so they dripped onto the wooden floorboards. We were cursing them, September said, her hair plastered to her head, her eyes full of candle flame.

The high street was open late on Thursdays and we went charity-shop cruising in search of a dress for Mum to wear at her book launch. She walked between September and me, chatting away. She had painted her mouth red for the outing and the cold made her eyes pink. She looked happy – the way she always did when a big project had been finished – and I considered, for a moment, telling her about the things that had been happening at school. We walked along the street, popping in and out of shops, passing our hands through the racks and then moving on. I closed my fingers around Mum's hand and thought of the way I would say it. Listen, I'm not happy. Ahead people were emptying onto the pathway and I saw – with a shock like electricity – the three girls in the crowd, their arms filled with bags, their flat faces and shiny hair, their leather jackets. I dropped behind Mum and September, thought: Do not see me do not see me do not do not do not. They were talking, their faces close together. Lily's mouth was moving fast, her hands gesticulating through the loops of the shopping

46

bags. We were nearly past them. The crowd was thick, the music from the shops turned up so loud that I could barely hear my own footsteps. I lowered my head. They were walking past. It's fine, I thought, I'm in the clear, and then Lily looked up and caught my eye and was gone. Did you see her? I said to September later but she only frowned at me, passed Mum something through the changing-room curtain.

Mum tried on dresses and we sat outside the changing rooms and said: No, no, maybe, no, maybe, what about ...? In the changing-room mirrors September looked bright, glowing through the second-hand clothes, the clogged bags of ancient jewellery and baskets of scratched records. I looked peaky and pale, grey around the edges like fruit on the turn. September wrapped scarves around my neck and loaded her fingers with rings and made the women running the charity shop shifty and angry. I thought about the girls and knew that by catching Lily's eye I had called something down upon myself.

September and Mum went through phases. Sometimes they were best friends and I would catch them giggling at the kitchen table, but often they were fraught and fought about small things, rubbed one another up the wrong way. There had been a cold snap at Christmas, frost on the ground, the car windscreen iced solid. A row over what to eat for dinner had picked up speed, turned into the two of them screaming at each other across the kitchen, September picking up a cup from the side and lifting as if to throw. Don't you dare, Mum had said, you just try it. Don't you dare. There had been

47

other arguments at the start of the year; those January days, barely even eight hours of light, the scurry of wind-thrown-leaves up and down the street, sudden harried bursts of rain which clogged the gutters and made the house smell of damp. There were disagreements over the dishes or what to watch in the evening, over the clothes September stole from Mum's wardrobe and then got food on. I placated or lied to prevent shouting matches, calmed September down. They were at cross purposes and I had worried, exhaustedly, about the clothes trip. But September was sweet and Mum was forgiving, their linked arms, the plaits September wove into Mum's hair. In the charity shop Mum tried on a gold dress with a wide skirt and a square neckline.

That one, September said so loudly that heads turned across the shop and Mum laughed and spun on the worn floorboards.

The next day I saw Lily everywhere. At a table near ours at lunchtime, whirling her spoon on the tray and looking over. In the toilets, passing one another by the mirror, Lily's shoulder missing mine by a whisker. There was swimming in the afternoon. The teacher was late, and we sat on the side of the pool and waited for her. Ryan was there with a group of friends, skinny in his red-spotted swimming trunks, goggles pushed onto the top of his head. September hummed in annoyance at the volume of his voice, the way he pretended to tackle one of the other boys towards the water. I watched. His dimpled smile and overgrown hair, his quick movements.

More than that. The shape of him in those trunks, the colour of his nipples, that black hair beneath his armpits, the small red spots that sometimes scattered his chin. The exactitude of him, the humanness. September whistled until I turned and then blinked at me. I had been staring. Over Ryan's shoulder – like a blood moon – Lily was watching me.

The teacher came in looking pissed off and asked us to draw the lane ropes down the pool from one end to the other. I was glad to move. I could feel Lily's gaze on the back of my head. I untangled the rope at the far end and pulled it along the tiled side. Watching my feet, avoiding the guttering, clogged with plasters and coils of hair that made my insides sink. There was noise at the end, a sort of rising sound, but I didn't look up. I was thinking about Ryan. Someone was there, moving past me, not far enough away. I was barged into and fell, the rope tangling around my ankles so that I did not fall far but into the water and sideways against the edge of the pool.

The medical bay was so clean it made my head feel white with emptiness. I thought about Mum's spinning gold dress and the way the water had turned murky as a Bloody Mary and I thought about the pieces that made up Ryan. Maybe I could just stay in the medical bay forever. September paced around, kicking at the floor and peering at the posters on the wall.

Look at this woman's nose, she said. It says cocaine melted it away.

The nurse had gone into the office and closed the door. September stole plasters and tiny bottles of antiseptic wash from the cupboards. The black lines on the bottom of the pool hovered in front of me. September came over and pressed her face to mine, muttered nonsense words into my ear.

Mum was there then, rushing through the door, car keys in hand, hair awry and wet at the ends, fingers stained with paint. She grabbed us and held on.

What happened? she asked once and then again in the car. But I wouldn't say and September wouldn't have told her even if I'd wanted her to. September didn't need anyone else. I knew only that if we told her it would get worse. Adults didn't understand. Adults had forgotten what it meant to be really afraid. In the rear-view mirror I caught her eye.

At home she brought down blankets and made us a fort on the sofa, sent September off to make cheese on toast. She perched on the side of the sofa and looked at me. There was charcoal on her face.

I know what will happen, she said.

It was not what I had expected. I sat very still and listened to the sound of September banging around in the kitchen. I waited for her to come back. She would know what to say.

I know what will happen, Mum said, if this gets out of control and September gets angry.

She pressed her fingers to my temple, rubbing at the taut skin. I leaned my head against her trousers, which smelled of graphite and black coffee. She had us with a man she had been afraid of, although she would not tell us why. There were months when she spoke little, only wanted to often be holding us, ordered takeaways, had baths that lasted all afternoon. There were months when she told us she was living in a sadness the colour of rust and leather.

I rubbed the material of her trousers between my fingers, opened and closed my mouth. There was nothing to say. I would not admit that September would fight them if she had to and that I would be glad when she did. I wondered, in that moment, what it was like to be a mother to children who did not need you.

September came stomping back in, mouth full of cheese, wide scowl.

That night September finished sentences for me, peeled us oranges to eat. Sometimes I would reach out to try and do something on my own and she would whistle and slap my hand down, turn the tap or pour the hot-chocolate mix into the cup herself. We huddled in our sofa fort and she fell asleep, exhausted, at nine o'clock with her head on my lap and the light from the TV turning her face green. It was then that the text came.

Saw you leaving today. Was worried. You OK?

It came from a number I didn't know because I didn't know anyone's besides Mum's and the number for the mobile September and I shared. I held the phone looking at the message and waiting for September to wake up and tell me what to do. I didn't know who it could be. We weren't friends with anyone at school, we avoided all contact. The one party Mum had arranged us an invitation to when we were seven ended in disaster when September cut off a girl's ponytail. I could think of no one who would have cared that I'd gone home early.

Who is this? I texted back.

The reply came immediately. My teeth clicked together. *Ryan*, and then there was a smiley face. *Is this July?*

Yes, I texted and then pushed the phone down the side of the sofa so I couldn't see it. Even then, sick with grim excitement, already set through with guilt at doing anything – let alone this – without September, I wondered if it wasn't him. But that night in bed, September sleeping on the other side of the room, I replied to the steady stream of texts that came in. Grew convinced that the words sounded like him, that there was something so distinctly Ryan-like about them as to make it impossible that it could be anyone else.

He wrote: *You're a good swimmer. I like swimming too, maybe sometime we should go together.*

He wrote: *Your sister is frightening! In a good way.*

He wrote: *We should talk more at school.*

At perhaps five o'clock he wrote: *Got to sleep. See you in 4 hours!*

It was the first abbreviation he'd used and it made me feel joyful.

The next day at school I watched him for signs of acknowledgement, but if he gave any, I did not see them. In maths he passed me a sheet of paper and smiled, perhaps. At lunchtime he let me take the last apple pie. September pulled my hair but didn't say anything.

4

Mum in her gold dress and red shoes borrowed from a friend. September doing my hair so that it lay flat against my head. The phone in the pocket of the dress I chose purposely. Mum so nervous that she drew her lipstick in an uneven line and September had to rub it off with tissue and redo it for her. Walking down into town with the big umbrella between the three of us, September's elbow in my ribs. The smell of Mum's perfume. The glow of the bookshop ahead of us, the square of light thrown onto the pavement when the door opened. The glasses of prosecco we drank quickly, timing one another.

The drawing on the front cover of Mum's latest book was of the two of us, September holding a compass and me behind her with an old-looking torch. We had been in her books for as long as I could remember. September had always liked that she drew us, that she could point to the books in the bookshop window and say that we were in them. I've never been certain. I didn't like the blank eyes of the page turned on me, the attention narrowed into a thin dart, the way people commented when they saw us in bookshops or at Mum's events. When I was five I wept and wept until Mum said she wouldn't draw me for a year and then the images had been only of September; scaling trees or swimming in the school pool to find a key that had dropped to the bottom and would open a locked box. Except a year later Mum was drawing me again and I'd felt – though silently this time – the same way.

The books were for children, with illustrations on every page. In the latest book we had escaped a nunnery and were trying to find our way into a secret cave where, supposedly, there was treasure. We wore matching yellow sashes (which we wore also for the launch) and September did all of the climbing and jumping and running while I was the researcher, head inside a book or behind an enormous magnifying glass. I had tried to read it but seeing my picture had made me feel light-headed so instead September read it aloud one evening, sprawled on Mum's bed while she worked upstairs. She did a funny accent when she spoke my lines, twisting her face in parody, making me wince.

Mum's publisher was at the party and so were her friends and most of the people from the bookshop. Everyone was talking, laughing. Someone had put on Kate Bush so loudly everyone had to yell to be heard. September threaded through the crowd, nicked glasses of wine and smiled charmingly when anyone looked her way. She was good at this. She always knew what to say. The phone went off in my pocket again and again. Mum would be doing a speech soon. We'd helped her write it the week before, drinking Earl Grey till late and laughing at her bad puns.

I slipped away from September and into the toilet. The floor was slick with sodden toilet roll. I sat on the loo seat.

Ryan said: *What you up to tonight?*

Ryan said: *I'm out with some friends. Wish you were here.*

Ryan said: *I feel as if no one really knows me. But I think maybe you do.*

At the end of each text he had put a smiley face and three kisses. The texts came through faster than I could reply to, slick with intent. My thumbs ached. When someone knocked loudly on the door I crouched on the floor, stayed silent. I told him about September and the launch and the book with us stolen into it. I told him about the things I worried about which I knew didn't mean anything but which I couldn't quite shake. He said: *I feel that way sometimes too.* He said: *That's funny! I think that as well.* Looking up, I became aware that it had been a long time since I'd left and that I would have missed the speeches.

When I went downstairs everyone was gone besides a few booksellers clearing away wine glasses.

They're in the pub, one said, pointing with his chin towards the door and the building over the road.

The pub was full so no one was sitting down, the chairs pushed against the walls, the staff sweating behind the long wooden bar, the floor slippery with spilled beer and crunchy with crushed handfuls of crisps. The music built in my eardrums to a roar. I wanted to take the phone outside and sit in the cold, wait for the texts to come through. I wanted to tell September what was happening and also to keep it to myself forever. I saw Mum at the bar, shoes in hand, laughing. A child went rushing past. September grabbed me by the arm and tugged me towards the exit. Someone came in and left the door ajar and the rain was driven against our legs.

Where were you? What were you doing? She was shaking me, teeth gritted, fingers clawed around the tops of my arms.

Nowhere.

I looked for you. I was looking for you for ages.

Sorry.

September let go of me, poked her tongue out. I needed you. Bloody hell.

Bloody hell, I said.

Fuck a duck.

In my pocket the phone vibrated. I have to go to the loo, I said.

No, you don't.

I do. I need to go.

She eyed me. You need to tell me what is going on.

I tried to make my brain as empty as possible. Nothing is going on.

I don't believe you.

I didn't say anything. If I said something then September would excavate between the words and find the truth buried there.

Have a drink and then you can go. She closed her hand around the top of my arm and tugged me towards a free corner, managed to persuade someone we were old enough to drink and we got a bottle of something sweet and sticky. She held it up to my mouth and I coughed through the bubbles. I could feel the phone in my pocket, tried to ignore it. September pointed out people we knew, leaned in to whisper in my ear.

I need a wee, I said. I could hear myself slurring a little, the words jumbling together.

She scowled at me, but when I pulled away she let me go.

The toilet was worse than the one in the bookshop. Someone was being sick in one of the cubicles and another of the toilets was blocked. I stood in front of the mirror and took the phone out of my pocket.

The text said: *I like you, July.*

I held on to the sink. I wrote a message (*I like you too*) and then deleted it, started another. A message came in.

I want to see you. Can u send a picture?

What sort of picture? I typed back though already I was going into the empty cubicle and locking the door, undoing my dress, holding the phone up away from me, my hands moving as if they belonged to someone else. The alcohol beat a second, greater certainty into me, I could feel it sloshing in my chest, making my fingers clumsy. The music upstairs boomed, thudded through the floor. I could already taste September's fury. There wasn't anything we didn't do together and yet here I was.

A sexy picture, the message said.

It took me a long time to get it right. I was so nervous that I kept dropping the phone or forgetting to smile. In most of them I looked frightened, as if kidnapped and forced to take the image by someone just out of sight of the camera. In all I looked haunted, barely there, ghostly the way I always felt in Mum's picture books. I kept thinking about September speaking the book aloud using my voice, a voice so convincing that I didn't even need to read my own parts. I thought: I need to go upstairs, get September, ask her to take it. But I didn't. The texts belonged to me and no one else.

Someone came into the bathroom and shouted my name.

July, where are you?

One moment, I said, fumbling at the phone, nearly dropping it, trying to take the photo. The door rattled, banged on its hinges. She was slamming on it with her fists. The bolt shuddered up and down. My teeth were gritted, I forced my eyes open wide, tugged my dress to the side, took one more photo and sent it.

Let me in, you she-witch.

I pulled the bolt back and she barrelled in, knocking me against the wall. Her pupils were blown, her mouth wet. She locked the door behind her.

What's going on?

Nothing, I said but my eyes moved to the phone and she grinned at me and went for it, grappling at my hands, scratching me on the face with her nails, almost getting

58

it. I jerked around, got myself in between her and it, shoved the loo seat up and dropped it in. She whistled as it sunk. No fun, July-bug.

The rest of the night was blurred, uneven. Mum got up on one of the old pub tables and made another speech in which she said there would be nothing without September and me. Someone yelled, Yeah, Sheela.

At two or three o'clock Mum got us chips from the takeaway near the house and we walked home. There was light from the moon. I thought of the eclipse/of zebra crossings/of the swimming pool where I had fallen and knocked my head. September was chattering on about the evening and Mum was laughing with her head tipped back and the chips were damp with vinegar and the phone was gone. Later I lay awake and then switched the light on. September had climbed into my bed and was sleeping with both arms flung above her head and her legs taking up more than half the space.

We were late for school. Mum was hung-over in sunglasses, drinking coffee from a Thermos, driving slowly. I took September's hand and tried to communicate silently what had happened, but she ignored me. She was still annoyed about the phone which she had insisted that we shared rather than having our own. I looked out of the window.

I just wish it would stop bloody raining, Mum said. The house is going to float away and take my darling girls with it.

The road outside the school was chock-a-block with traffic and we got out and walked up. I could feel the static in my fingers. The unease was like a half-digested meal. I took September's hand again and, that time, she must have felt something because she turned to look at me.

What is it? July-bug?

I shook my head. There were other girls waiting outside the school and they were looking over at us, their faces close together, their mouths wide dark organs peeling out of their skin.

What, July? September said but by then we were near the front of the school and, before I could think or speak, we were inside. There were people everywhere on their phones. Someone saw us and I heard my name being spoken and then repeated. September's face was changing. A teacher was pushing towards us, sweat marks in the armpits of her shirt, her hands raised, shoving us back out, but not before someone – over her shoulder – flashed a phone screen towards us and I could see it. I did not recognise the round face in it, the nipples like upturned exclamation marks in the centre of the screen. In the background of the photo was the top of the toilet cistern and the figure was wearing my dress. Every face was turned towards me, mooned globes in the stricken light of the corridor. It felt as if material had been shoved into my ears and nose and mouth and was swelling, sodden, beneath the skin; my teeth were hurting, as if I'd bitten into something very cold. September took in the photo and then turned and looked straight at me.

5

We took the week off and, every day, I watched September getting angrier, the way she drove through meals barely breathing. She made up a whole list of words to describe Lily, Kirsty and Jennifer: judderingwitches, ranksaliva-faces. I moved in a daze, from bed to sofa and back again, and September raged around me like a dog, raw with fury. Mum would come into the room with a suggestion for a film we could watch and September would look at her as if even she needed to keep away, as if even she should watch out. At night I would wake and Mum would be in the room with us, sitting in a chair by the window looking out at the street or turned towards the bed to watch us sleep. And I understood that she could only come close when September was asleep, made docile by unconscious-ness. She kept asking how I felt, how I was doing. I didn't want to talk about it, didn't want to make it any more certain. There were waves of realisation and with them a depth of alarm that was unfamiliar in its enormity.

*

The day before we went back to school September said we were going out and we walked into the centre and roamed around the shops. I was worried we would see people from school so she decked me out in a cap and sunglasses, swung our arms between us. We went into clothes shops and touched everything we could see, feeling the sequins, the soft folds of velvet. In Boots we tried on lipstick, crouched down so no one could see us. We sprayed perfume into the air and then stepped into the mist. I could feel the next day hanging in the over-lit aisles, beside the deodorant and shampoo bottles. Everyone who had seen the photo would be there and, also, worse, Ryan would be there too. Was it possible he hadn't seen it? Perhaps he had fallen sick and been off school. September dabbed perfume onto my neck and pulse points, said, I like this one and then put it into the pocket of my coat and made me walk out ahead of her through the doors.

It was a Monday and I could tell September wasn't going to let what had happened with the photo lie. She was so angry my head felt busy with it, with the planning. Mum must have sensed it too because she pulled over and leaned back to look at us.

It was awful, she said, but it's done now. Let's leave it there. She was looking at both of us but I knew that she wasn't talking to me. September knocked the door open, swung her feet out and was gone.

*

It was worse than it had been before. I was so used to melding with the walls, people seeming not to see me as they passed. That was broken now, the photo kept reappearing; someone photocopied it and stuck it up on the lockers in the senior common room, another person had emailed it around on the school computers so that we would see flashes of it wherever we went. I kept crying in class and having to go to the toilet, September hustling behind me. In the photo I looked like someone else and at times it was almost possible to think this was true; except then someone would point at me and I would remember. My stunned, flash-lit stare, my breasts. That was it. The part of me no one besides September had seen since I was a child.

Ryan had been called in to the Head's office. We saw him everywhere, like a burn against the pale yellow school hallways, at the end of corridors or coming out of classrooms we were about to go into, in the sports hall with his skinny legs cutting out from beneath his shorts. Of course he had seen it and of course he knew that I had taken it thinking I was sending it to him. He probably hadn't even acknowledged who I was before but he did now.

Everyone who knew anything knew it wasn't him. It was clear in the way Lily and the two other girls walked. In the way they laughed whenever I came into a room. One morning Kirsty had got a copy of the picture and paraded around with it attached to her chest. It was before class and there was fog at all of the windows. We were sitting in the common room waiting for registration. Ryan was over by the lockers, leaning, arms folded, chuckling at something that someone had just said to him. Kirsty had her hair in small Princess Leia buns and her blazer flung over one arm. The photo was stuck with Sellotape to the front of her white shirt and kept sliding off so she held it in place with her fingernails which were painted green. Behind her I could see Jennifer and some other girls cracking up, bent double while people turned to see what they were laughing about. I mined my teeth down into the soft meat of my bottom lip and repeated: don't don't don't don't. September's anger was breaking out of her face, like shards of wood. She was rising off the bench we were sitting on. I reached out for her blindly, anguished. She pushed me away. Kirsty's eyes were flicking towards us, watching September warily, as if she was beginning to regret her decision. September grasped Kirsty by one of her buns and tugged her head down towards the floor while Kirsty yelped and clawed at her. There was a wrestle for control, Kirsty screaming (Let me go, you fucking whore) and everyone else piling in. Ryan and some of his friends had got up on the pool table to watch. Half the class were in the melee, grappling, pulling at September's hair and arms, grabbing at my face. I could feel the scream shuddering around my ribs, threatening to emerge. A teacher waded in and got hit, his nose started to bleed. September was wrenched away and Kirsty came after, rushing, fists raised and flailing. I put my hands either side of my face and forced inwards as hard as I could.

*

They were suspended for three days and I wouldn't go to school without September. Mum didn't make me. September's thoughtful face at the kitchen table, drinking coffee and doing the homework they'd sent. I wasn't sleeping and she stayed awake with me. We played September Says and hide-and-seek, like children in the darkness, ferreting around on hands and knees, smearing the dust from behind the sofa onto our faces. She kept saying: I'm going to do something about it. I didn't know what she meant and I was afraid to ask. She had acted this way before, in retribution or anger, and it had never ended well. The time when we were very young and another child had stolen my bag and she'd glued their hands to the table, the moments when Mum disagreed with her and she got that look on her face.

I thought up other options, other ways out. We could leave and never come back. We could change our names so no one would know us. The three of us could go to Iceland or Mexico. I almost said these things to her but always something stopped me. I kept forgetting what had happened and then, with a cold shudder, would remember all over again.

I know what we can do, she said one afternoon. On the radio it said a storm called Regina was moving down the country towards us. She tapped her fingers at the windy street beyond the glass. You remember the place by the old tennis courts? That weird storage shed.

We had been there a couple of times when we first joined the school, looking for somewhere to hide out.

The tennis courts were in occasional use then but the shed was already softening and mouldy and over the years the trees had grown up around the courts and hidden them from view of the field. They weren't used any more. September switched on the bedside lamp. The light seemed to bounce off her eyes.

I thought maybe we could go there and tell Lily and the others to come.

I didn't say anything.

What do you think?

I stayed quiet.

Come on. Don't be a pain, she said. We'll get them to meet us there and then I'll talk to them, away from everyone else. I'll warn them off.

I'm not being a pain.

You are.

My saliva tasted stale. It's a good idea.

I know, she said. So, I'll ask them tomorrow?

OK, I said.

What did you say?

OK, I said loudly.

Everything had been leading there: the old tennis courts swimming with water from the storm, our muddy feet and hands, the ancient floodlights groaning under the weight of the wind. September whistled a pied piper's tune and even through the gusts and rain I could hear it, calling me. In the kitchen I'd watched her slip Mum's sharp onion-chopping knife into her pocket and then square her chin at me, daring me to say something. At the tennis court a tree had fallen – had it? – weakened by the deluge, and the shed buckled beneath it. I'd been able to hear the ambulance, the rain must have abated. Mum's hands on the steering wheel were white-knuckled. September said into my ear that there was nothing I could have done and it had to happen the way it did. My memory is hazy. The girls, gathered on the turning circle, looked frightened. All in all, I hadn't been able to see why there was such a fuss made. We'd put the wind up them. That's all that had really happened, September said. We'd put the wind right up them.

Afterwards I came down with something. Not one of the colds I would have all through the winter and into the chilly spring but a harsher illness. I was sick often in the frigid mornings, throwing up whatever I'd had for dinner, and the skin on my hands and the backs of my legs grew sore and red, peeled off or itched so much I'd sometimes wake in the night and have scratched myself to bleeding. I was tired and the pills the doctor had prescribed made me more tired and irritable, often dazed.

We'd made a pact. Back in Oxford. Hand in hand in front of the mirror to double-check with our reflections that the promise would hold true. We would weather whatever was going to come. September stood next to me but, still, it felt as if my hand closed around nothing. I squeezed and squeezed. July, she said, do you promise? I would promise her anything. July, she said, listen to me. We'd never broken a promise to one another before.

6

Something is crouched on top of me as I sleep. I cannot open my eyes. There is breath on my face, hot, and the grind of what feels like fists on my chest. I try to speak, call for September, but I can't move, my arms and legs are stiff by my sides. I can open an eye, just a little, a blurred view. There is a figure above me, bearing down, their face is almost recognisable but then there is darkening and they are gone.

Mum has been down in the night and there is a saucepan of chilli on the side with a heart of coriander leaves on top. September sniffs at it and then refuses to eat. I fill a bowl almost to the rim, watch it revolving through the door of the microwave, burn the roof of my mouth shovelling it in. Eat another bowl as soon as I've finished the first. My chest is painful, beginning to bruise. The marks frighten me, the splayed, finger-like shape of them. I want to ask September but she seems pent up. She logs us on to a few of the chat sites we've been on before so we can check our profiles, and there are some messages. Sometimes we tell ourselves stories about these imaginary women we create. We think of what they did at school, who their friends were, what they do at the weekend. We imagine small pockets from their lives: the time they rescued a cat on holiday in Greece, the best meal they ever had. It makes me nervous going on the site, pretending, the lurking possibility that we might be found out. Sometimes we pretend to be men instead and that is easier, so far from who we really are. Pretending to be someone else is like wearing an outfit that does not quite fit, the sleeves leaving red marks around the arms, the waistband sagging.

There is something wrong with the Internet. Pop-ups crowd our screen and the laptop lets out a low, unhappy whirring noise. The sites we want to visit are missing whole chunks, photographs appear decimated, sentences end in the middle. We persist for longer than we should and finally all our tabs close at once and we are ejected onto a black screen.

Viruses are ghosts on the Internet, September says and then, shoulders hunched nearly to her chin, mutters: Fuck, fuck, fuck. Let's go to the beach.

We stand for a time outside Mum's bedroom. When I put my ear against the wood I think I can hear her moving about inside, almost rodent-like, scuttling. I listen for the noise of pencils on paper. If she is working then everything will be fine. There was a new book she had started just before we left Oxford. In it September

69

and I took a boat to an island covered in snow, even though it was the middle of summer, and tried to return it to warmth. If she is working perhaps she can forgive us. But, after the initial movement, there is mostly silence.

Come on, September says, we'll leave her a note.

Though in the end we do not do even that. There are too-big wellies at the back door which we push our feet into. September is turning out the front of the house, arms akimbo, chin tipped back towards the sky that is, almost, steely blue. There is something around her neck, flying with her. The binoculars. I had not seen her take them from the house.

Why have you brought those?

Why do you think? she says, her voice refracting and rising as she whirls.

I remember the time Mum had come back from a dinner party at a friend's house, her tongue loosened, made us hot chocolate in the kitchen. She'd told us about our father and the binoculars he'd had since he was a child, how he had been possessive of them, furious if he caught her touching them. The times he'd wrapped up, put the binoculars around his neck and gone out bird hunting. That's what he'd called it, not watching, but hunting. He came back electric, chattering on. I think of him standing at one of the windows above our heads and watching us through his binoculars. He is young, younger than us even, and the raw skin around his September-blue eyes is marked with red from pressing the binoculars in.

70

September is marching down the lane, her calves lifting out of the too-big boots. I rush to catch up and we walk for a few paces in step, our arms next to one another.

Look, September points. The horizon jiggles with the hills but there, in the distance, is a line of sea. It is the end of May and the sun is warm on our heads, the smell of hot earth. At times I feel resistance within me, like finding – blind – the beginning of a drop with your toes. I try and add weight in my hands but she pulls me onwards. I think of Mum coming out of the bedroom to find us gone. It would not be impossible for her to think that we had run away, left her forever. We are speeding up, plummeting off the road and into a field, the grass thick and sharp, nearly drawing blood. September hesitates, clamps the binoculars to her eyes and swivels her head to stare up at the sky.

What are you looking at?

She doesn't answer.

I move further up towards the dunes ahead. September is making sounds behind me, clicking, odd calls, muttered incantations, made-up words. The sea looks greasy, slicked with white. A track down towards the beach. I take off my wellies, the ground is damp and chilly and then hot and dry.

I look back; September is gone from the sandy drop beneath me. I stumble along the top of the dune looking for her. Ahead there is a flash of something, a shape, a building on the dune, built on stilts up off the sand. There is a thin, glassless window, barely bigger than my flattened palm, that runs all around its circumference.

There is someone inside, looking out at me. I do not know who it is but it is not September. I hunker down, try to make myself small on the ground. The ray of the narrow window holds me in place. An entrance in the side is opening outwards slowly. I understand that whoever comes out will explain everything about what happened at the tennis court.

What are you doing? September shouts. She is holding on to the door frame into the wooden box and leaning out. The binoculars hang from her neck towards the ground. What are you doing out there? Come in.

No, I say and see the flicker of her acknowledging my dissent; that will have repercussions later.

It's a birdwatching box. I think I saw a kite. Or a heron. Come in.

I thought we were going to the sea, I say. That's what you said. We were going to the sea.

I straighten with difficulty and skid down away from the box and towards the beach. September is shouting and laughing behind me. The slope is steep and I go down on my backside towards the long beach and the freezing waves. The tide is out and there is a scud of rubbish and debris on the sand. I heave myself up and take the last of the slope at a run, September coming behind me, cackling. I feel better when I can't see the box. September wraps her arms around me from behind and I think that maybe she has forgiven me.

We trek up and down the beach. Occasionally the sun comes out and throws long shadows onto the tiny stones, beats down onto our shoulders. Mostly, though, there is a tough wind and the sand is brought against our bare legs, our hair salty in our mouths. September lies down and I bury her, one limb at a time and then her torso. She looks like a sea creature, sandy-haired.

Someone's coming, she says. I turn and look into the wind. There's a figure at the other end of the beach, clambering along the outcrop of rock. A body wearing an orange anorak.

Shall we leave? I say but September doesn't hear or, if she does, doesn't answer. The figure is close now and I can see his face, make out the colour of his hair, bright like his coat. The waves are moving up the beach.

Hello, he shouts, calling until he's close enough to stop. Hi. He's got what I think must be a local accent and is our age or a little younger, both hands buried to the wrists in his pockets, a wide mouth.

Hi, I say.

Behind me September mutters something and starts to dig herself out like a turtle. He smells of sea salt and shampoo. He takes his arms out of his pockets and moves them back and forth. He is long-limbed and awkward-looking, tufts of hair sticking up across his scalp.

You live around here then? he says. I haven't seen you before.

I don't know what to say. There is something about him.

We just moved here, September says over my shoulder. He smiles, clacks his tongue. Cool, that would be why I haven't seen you. Where do you live?

I point off the beach towards the house and September says, Over there. In the Settle House.

Really? he says.

Yes, she says.

We're having a party tonight.

What sort of party? September says, rude, her voice louder than necessary.

A beach party. No one comes here this early in the year. We'll light a fire, have some beers. You should come.

I wait for September to speak but she is silent.

OK, I say slowly. Maybe.

Good, he says. Good. We'll be here tonight.

I watch him trudging away up the beach, head lowered against the wind. When I turn around September is looking at me, brushing the sand off her hands, shaking it from her hair.

I didn't mean to, I say. We don't have to.

We should. Come on. Let's decide what to wear before you change your mind.

We find the box of bottles Mum hasn't unpacked yet and sip from an old one. It says Port on the label but mostly it tastes of dust.

Do you feel anything? I say.

No, September says and shrugs.

I feel a bit wobbly but I won't admit it if September won't.

We parade upstairs and lay out dresses. September twizzles with her arms raised. I feel bursts of anxiety

beneath my chest and hold my breath, waiting for them to go away. September puts her arms around my neck.

Don't worry, July-bug, it'll be fine. You might even have fun. Let's put some music on.

But the Internet is still playing up and the music comes through only intermittently, whining and then dropping away. We switch it off.

Wear this one, September says holding up a dress with a high lace collar and spaghetti bolognese staining the hem.

I don't want to.

Put it on, you'll feel better.

I feel a tinge of annoyance at her but do as I am told. September is in her bra and underwear doing headstands against the side of the bed. I put my cheek against the wall and wait for the house to speak, to comment on the party and the red-headed boy, but, if it does, I don't hear it.

We look in the kitchen for something to eat, but there is only leftover chilli and tea bags.

Eating is cheating anyway, September says. We'll get drunker if we don't bother.

We swallow glasses of water instead, drinking until our stomachs are swollen out of their ribcages, burbling watery, made-up words at one another.

7

By the time we reach the track down to the beach it is dark. The night is different from Oxford where the sky is stained with pollution, street lamps lining the roads. It is so dark I can barely make out September moving a couple of paces ahead. Only know that she is there by the feel of her hand, fingers opening and closing around my own. I wait to see the wooden bird-viewing box rising up from the sands but we have come a different route and it is not there. The relief at not seeing the bird box is swallowed, soon, easily, by trepidation. We should go back to the house. Of course we should. The beach is below us, a fire, the sound of voices carried upwards, the sound of the sea which is both too loud and too distant, as if we will never reach it. There are people around the fire, leaping from one side to the other. We shouldn't. But September only intensifies her grip around my hand and tugs until we are running down the track.

We don't go straight to the group but circle it, out of sight in the dark.

September holds our shoes above her head and the sea comes cold over our bare ankles. I feel the rim of my dress dragging in the water and hitch the long tail over one arm. There is the smell of beer and of something burning. I can see September's eyes glowing like a caught-out animal, turning towards the fire and the people sat around it. We move closer slowly. There are six figures in a loose ring, our age, drinking from cans of beer and talking over one another. A few have wet hair as if they've been in the sea. One of them sees us and raises his hands, waves.

Hi, he says. The rest turn to look our way.

September gives me a push and we are moving forward into the light. There is a hunk of meat cooking, singed to black, and a couple of empty tins shoved in among the ashes. They're burning driftwood and there is the sizzle of salt. One of the girls chucks a beer and it strikes my leg and falls to the sand where September picks it up and holds it to my mouth so there isn't anything I can do but drink. Someone around the fire whoops and someone else laughs. The beer is warm.

You came, the boy we had met before says. It is that mouth, perhaps. Or the way he talks. His accent thick enough it takes me a while to get the words.

Said so, September says and then sits close to the fire. I fold down just behind her. The people say their names but I don't remember any of them a moment later besides his which is John. There are two boys and the rest are girls. I say my name and hear September, like an echo, saying her own. One of the girls – silver metal in her nose – asks us why we moved here.

Why not? September says and, in the silence, other conversations start up around us. They talk about people they all know, things that happened at school. Someone gives me another beer though I can't remember finishing the first. The other boy makes jokes that no one really laughs at while John talks to me so quietly I can barely hear him. I think: September September September and find her still sitting next to me, not drinking only looking into the fire. John is on my other side. I feel him shift closer so that his arm is touching mine. I think: what am I going to do? I can feel the slow current passing from him to me. I think, in that moment, that he must be able to tell my thoughts the way I can sometimes tell September's, through the skin, like electrical wire.

I take whatever is offered: a burnt bit of what might be chicken, a bottle of cider that I taste and then leave by my side for September to drink which she does. They ask us more questions: Where were we before? What school do we go to? And September answers: We were in Oxford before. We aren't going to school.

You aren't going to school? the other boy says. Why not?

Because we don't want to, she says and grins at them. Because we don't do anything we don't want to.

No one has anything to say to that although one of the girls raises her beer can towards us.

John is speaking and I turn so I can hear. He's talking faster than I can keep up with, telling some story that I can't concentrate on. I can feel the beer and the cider

78

and the port in my head and in my hands, which I raise to my face to check aren't shaking. September has gone quiet next to me. John puts his face close to mine and for a moment I feel his mouth on my cheek; it is almost too much to stand. I pull back and look at him. Do it again, I think. Do it again. But I don't say anything.

We keep drinking. I check often to see that September is there and she smiles at me and touches my face and hair, holds my hands and moves them towards bottles of beer, bottles of sugary cider. The conversations run around us like a river with us catching only occasionally on loose, unstuck phrases or questions directed not at us but in our general direction. I find myself talking or look and see that September is talking for the both of us. She is, at times, sharp and mean the way I know her to be when around anyone but me – and occasionally Mum – but at other moments she seems to soften towards them, these strangers, and I hear her talking about what our mum does and the things we are interested in. And, looking across the fire, I see how they lean close to her to hear and nod or laugh in agreement and ask her more questions or say something to try and draw her approval. I am drunk. Yes. I think then, as I have so many times, she is the person I have always wanted to be. I am a shape cut out of the universe, tinged with ever-dying stars – and she is the creature to fill the gap I leave in the world. I remember the promise we made years ago, how we'd written it down so we wouldn't forget, how we'd linked hands and held them over the paper and squeezed and squeezed.

I find myself down by the water. I am drunk and September has pulled her dress up over her head and her body flashes like a lighthouse in the dim. The sea is beating cold against my calves. The bottom of my dress grows sodden and is drawn against my skin. There are figures further out in the spume of spray, throwing their backs against the crest of the waves. One of the boys is naked and I see his penis against his thigh, rising out of the water as he jumps.

I feel the change before I see it. A tingling in my fingers, I am crying though I cannot tell why. I take a step back. When I say September's name I think I hear an answering call but I am not certain. It seems so far off, an impossible distance. Someone is touching me though I cannot see their hands or face. I look towards the fire but there is no one there. None of the people are John. I move along the beach, feeling too drunk, as if I have too many limbs, tens of thousands of toes. I call September's name and someone laughs. Someone is holding my wrist. Then I see her, just lit by the fire. She is walking away. She has put her dress back on and it clings to her. There is someone with her. It is John. The fire moves, changes, and for a moment the shadows of September and the person with her are huge, monstrous. I retreat to the flames. I am so cold I can't feel my extremities; my fingers are numb from tip to knuckle bone. My hands feel full, when I try to clench them shut they won't close. For a startling second I am uprooted, displaced. I can feel September's fingers within my own, a double heartbeat starting like a blip in my chest, my mouth so full with a second tongue that I cannot breathe. I lie back on the sand. There is a slowing down, as if the world starts to drag. There is a tightening and then in my crotch a pressure, sudden, startling, too fast to be really painful. It is cold wherever September is. September, I think. September September September. There is something leaving me. I feel it seeping away, going going gone. There is pain, then, and I bite my tongue and taste salt and iron. There is pain which makes me think that perhaps I am with September and John, curled inside her, watchful, feeling what is going on. There is something leaving me and I realise with a shock that it is my virginity. Going going gone. Taken in a second-hand way. September is having sex and – because really two means one – I am having sex too. I close my eyes, ball my fists into the sand.

PART TWO

The Settle House

At the start there was only earth where the house would be. Strong trees made to survive the sea winds, the dirt sodden and salted, teeming with life. Sheep grazed on the hills, gave birth, died, filled the ground with themselves. Small settlements, shepherds' bothies, fishermen's huts, travellers' vardos, the stench of bass and wrasse, cod and whiting laid out to dry. Moles strung from the fence posts to save the fields. Rabbit traps with biting mouths. Whales beached themselves onto the stones and were laid waste to by the elements. The people did what they always did, lived and lived and lived and bled and were ended.

The Settle House is built although it hasn't yet found its name. Everything flurries and barks and continues around it. People in the nearest village watch the house going up, watch how the build stutters, nearly fails, grinds on. This sandy earth consumes buildings like that. Yet it stands and people come and go from inside its walls.

September and July's father, Peter, is conceived in the house. The walls shudder, do not turn away. It is done quickly. In the murky womb something flickers to life, small, easily extinguishable. Peter's parents pack up and go home to Denmark. The house is alone again. Mice breed like rabbits beneath the floorboards, birds nest and mate in the roof, a badger digs a sett by the far wall and then abandons it for a better place. There are holidays in the house, sandwiches more sand than bread, chilly forays into the miserable sea. Peter is given a pair of binoculars for his birthday and watches birds from the house's windows, their stacking alignment in the sky. Ursa is conceived in the house. Peter thinks: I don't want a sister. The locals in the village think: they'll sell up and be gone soon. The house springs leaks, clogged gutters, squeaky doors. Sometimes Peter takes the baby out to the beach and leaves it in the sand, watches the sea coming in.

Time loses its line and jiggles out of place. Everyone is living and dying at the same moment. The house has been standing for nearly fifty years, the foundations have only just been laid, the land is bare and barely good even for farming. There are whales on the beaches.

Peter thinks: what would a shithole place like this sell for?

Ursa thinks: I'll never come back here.

Sheela thinks: I'll never come back here.

September thinks: I wish July would –

July thinks: I don't want to –

*

There are crusts of moths growing and spiders in their wintery sacks. There are the bones of tiny animals in the foundations. There are nettles in the garden, their roots tangling labyrinthine in the dirt. Ursa fights her brother in the house and loses a fingernail beneath the kitchen counter, her teeth stained with blood. Sheela dreams of her unborn children in the house, sees them as tiny smudges of charcoal on the walls. When the house is empty – as it often is – the villagers sometimes break a window and drink in the low-ceilinged living room, drop their beer cans into the fireplace, conceive their own children in the beds, leave their footprints high up on the walls. Peter is a child turning his binoculars to the sea, looking for drowning boats. Sheela is giving birth in the still bedroom, the house frozen around her, watchful as a child. Sheela and Peter are having sex in the bath, the water soaking the floor, Sheela's fingers bent at an angle in his mouth. Peter and Ursa's parents are having sex in the bedroom, the duvet pulled over their heads, the light filtered red. Sheela and Peter are fighting in the kitchen, a glass hits the wall and explodes outwards, their eyes are closed, the glass is caught in the moment before breaking, Sheela is holding it in her hand, raising it up to drink. The house is straining to see down to the beach where September and July are up to their waists in the sea, the fire on their faces.

Sheela

1

She has always known that houses are bodies and that her body is a house in more ways than most. She had housed those beautiful daughters, hadn't she, and she had housed depression all through her life like a smaller, weightier child, and she housed excitement and love and despair and in the Settle House she houses an unsettling worry that she finds difficult to shake, an exhaustion that smothers the days out of her.

There are so many noises she cannot sleep. In the night, mostly, thumps and thundering, the sound of many footsteps, the crash of windows opening and closing, sudden explosions which sound like shouting. Sometimes she goes rushing out, still half asleep, but there is never anyone there. At times, awoken in the darkness, she thinks again about how that house is, more than any other, a body. She remembers feeling the same when she'd first been there, filled up with September – an inelegant pregnancy Peter had said, pointing at the women on the street who, from behind, did not seem pregnant at all – and alert almost all of the time to small changes. In the temperature, in the smells of the house, in the way the air seemed to fill the rooms. She was eight months when they moved here, maybe more, and she got hot easily, liked and disliked different foods strongly every day, sometimes could barely stand to be in a room for no reason at all. By the time September was due, a few days late, she had become convinced that the house was like her, a shifting and changing thing, awkward in its flesh, sometimes swelling and bloating out from its own walls, sometimes growing so warm the sweat pooled in her eyes.

She was in contact with no one from Peter's family aside from Ursa and even then rarely. There were cards for the girls on their birthdays and sometimes they met for lunch in grim roadside pubs between their two houses but there was little love lost. Only the imperative of family. Sheela knew that Ursa – although her tense politeness would never allow her to say so – blamed her in part for Peter's death, for taking the children away from him when they were babies, for not sticking it out. For the three years before the girls were born they'd sometimes taken holidays together, the three of them, stayed in cheap cottages in Wales or Scotland. Peter had gone off with his binoculars and the two women would sit at the greening tables outside the cottages and sometimes Ursa would tell her the way it had been when they were children; the moments of small violence that dominated their relationship. Although when he was back she would rush around after him, make him food, bring him presents, fight for his approval in a way that, worryingly, Sheela saw herself beginning to do too. He was like a black hole and nothing caught in his gravitational pull could survive for long. They'd been together for five years before she left and every year – especially once the girls were born – she'd thought: this one, time to go, this one.

A year after he'd died there had been the phone call in the night, Ursa's tremulous voice rising and falling through the static. I couldn't tell you until now, I'm sorry, he's dead, that's all there is to it. Sheela had not blamed her for waiting so long. She understood what it was like to both love and hate Peter.

After everything that had happened at the school it was Ursa she had rung. She owned the cottage in Yorkshire where Sheela had given birth to September and where they had gone after a particularly bad year when the girls were young and when Sheela told her what she needed she had said, without hesitation, yes and phoned the tenants to give them notice.

Footsteps in the night, doors that she was certain she had closed standing open, the boiler always on even when she turned it off, the Internet so slow she could barely send an email. She was rebelling against herself, refusing her meaningful living, and the house was doing the same, shutting down like an ancient computer.

One night a bang like someone falling. Her feet tangling in the cord of her dressing gown and nearly felling her, grabbing the glass on her bedside table in case she needed a weapon. Peering down the stairs; there was a light on in the sitting room. She stood swivelling in the murky gloom, searching. Nothing there, nobody broken in to kill them. A creasing in the air like the moment just after a train has passed and she is certain that it is Peter. Come back or there all along. And then the room seemed to lessen again and she knew she was tired and grieving something that had been lost. She switched the lights off, climbed back up the stairs and fell into bed.

When they were very young. Her two girls. One chasing the other out. Those early days when July was just born and September not quite a year and their father had been gone maybe a week or so. The room in Oxford where they lived for a while, mostly in the bed, the smell of breast milk and old cups of herbal tea, the picture books she read to September, July tucked in the crook of her arm. She'd never had so many hands on her, feeling like her skin could wear away like thin material. Her love for them was like carrying shopping bags up a hill and at times she became convinced they wanted the very foundations of her, wanted to break the bricks of her body apart and climb back in.

And earlier, in the Settle House, September just born and Peter like a ship on fire in the night, sails alight and taking all the other boats with it. His fingers closed around her wrists, his voice in the language she did not know but that he used all the same. She had told him before that he had to leave and this time she had done it with her fists thudding against his face. After he was gone she hid the key in the back of the drawer or underneath the mattress or in the pocket of her pyjamas and sometimes she was woken in the night by the sound of him trying to get in, not shouting but moving quietly around the outside of the house, searching for an entrance. Later – when he would try to get into the house in Oxford – she would lie across the threshold of their room like a wolf mother, listen to the sound of them having the same dream, talking in their sleep. What would she dream if she could? Of the days she had loved him, of the shape of his hands, of the pressure inside her of two daughters she sometimes wondered if she should not have had. Love was not enough in the end, not that kind of love.

Before July was even born she would take September in the buggy to the university parks and September would hold her head against Sheela's pregnant front and murmur noises.

What's that? What are you saying?

And September would grin and pat Sheela.

Your sister.

Smiling her gappy smile.

She could not have guessed the way they would be. Out in the garden in the white dresses they had begged her to buy from a charity shop, their muddy knees, their faces close together. They always seemed to be telling some great secret, some truth only they could know. The look in their eyes when she came across them, the sudden silence that fell and that she could not quite break into. The sound of her banal chatting as she tried to befriend them. Her own children. The things the teachers said about them at school: isolated, uninterested, conjoined, young for their age, sometimes moved to great cruelty. September's and July's faces as she scolded them, the looks they threw at one another. They had tried to flush a boy's pet hamster down the toilet, they had revealed to a child that her parents were divorcing, to another that Father Christmas wasn't real.

The way they ate. September had always been picky, refusing anything green or red or yellow, somehow always knowing when Sheela had blended vegetables or mashed them in, screaming and screaming until the plate was taken away. July was different, voracious, happiest when munching carrot sticks or grapes, face smeared, gummy smile. She would catch September whispering to baby July or pushing the vegetable-filled plate away from her hands. July also beginning to refuse food. By the time September was five and July a year younger they had become bizarrely selective, seemingly without logic or order; one week nothing but pancakes, the next only satsumas and chopped, peeled apples. In a particularly difficult week she fought with them to make them eat anything but jelly babies. The doctor had said it was stubbornness and if one broke then the other would follow and she thought this was true. It had affected July more than her sister, made her suspicious of anything that wasn't made at home, made her wan and thin-haired. September was the ringleader but July was the one who suffered. Later they were better but still mostly they loved cheese sandwiches – sometimes, but rarely, with onion or mayonnaise in – the crusts cut away, chopped into easily devourable triangles.

They were so young. At ten and eleven they seemed barely older than six, the curls of their childlike language, the ribbons they insisted she plait into their hair. As teenagers it had been even more noticeable, how different they were from the other children at school; clever but stunted, naive, happily young. Often she wondered if they held one another inside of childhood, arms around each other, clinging on.

The Halloween September was thirteen. Both of them suddenly grown long, limbs flung all over the place, mouths jammed with tangles of teeth, hacking at a pumpkin on the kitchen table. She'd started initiating separate dinner plans with them both, once every other week. One would be left at home and she'd take the other for noodles or to the cinema. It enraged September who would often refuse to speak, chomp away at her food; but she thought maybe July quietly liked it, a chance to speak about school or the books she was reading without September's voice overlaying her own. They had never celebrated Halloween before but the girls had got into horror films and been planning for months what they would do. The house was speckled with hanging spiders and fake cobwebs, buckets of squashy eyeballs. She tripped over a cheap plastic broom-stick in the hallway. They were in the kitchen with the pumpkin spread over the walls, witch hats shoved onto their heads.

Maybe I could come with you, she said at six thirty when they were lighting the candles for the pumpkin, putting on their outfits.

Maybe not, September said. July's face was pained. Sheela wished she hadn't said anything, had known better. The night before September had come up behind her and wrapped her arms around her middle, squeezing in a way she hadn't done since she was five. The relief of it had made her think she could overstep the carefully laid-out boundaries.

Someone, said July – ever the peacekeeper – needs to stay here to give out the sweets.

At seven o'clock they went trick-or-treating and she left the house in secret and walked a safe distance behind them. She lingered behind hedges and watched them approach houses, July's head tipped towards September's, listening. They had dressed as the sisters from *The Shining*, powdered their faces with flour, curled their hair; they would never look the same – July was too like her and September too like her father for that – but there was something about the way they moved that was disconcerting, like unfinished doppelgängers, turning their heads at the same time. There weren't many other children out but there were a few and she watched July and September plotting tactics, peering into small chil-dren's buckets to see if somewhere was worth visiting.

It got darker and she could shift closer, sometimes hear the things they said to each other, the clink of sweets in the mixing bowl July was carrying around. She wanted very desperately to move into the pool from street lamps and walk with them but she kept away, tailed them doggedly, paused as they knocked and came out cackling with glee at what they had got. They went up the long path to a house and she leaned against the wall and gazed away down the street at the bikes chained up, the rattle of a bus. When she turned back, they were gone. She walked swiftly but she could not find them. By a lamp post she found their bowl of sweets, set down. She panicked, then, and ran around, asked some passing people, thought of calling the police and, instead, ran back to check the house. Went shouting through the rooms. Turned around to see September standing in the open doorway, alone, her face wiped clean, expectant.

July is gone, she thought. I shouldn't have looked away. I knew this would happen.

Where – she started to say and then July was there, smiling, saying that they'd lost all the sweets, never mind.

Never mind, she said, reaching out for her, for them.

Afterwards – and she hated herself for the thought – she wondered if September had orchestrated it. That difficult, wonderful child who had fought her since she was born, refused food, ignored her breast, hated any of the toys she bought, who knew just how to antagonise her without, it seemed, even trying. Had she, in fact, known that she was following them and planned every-thing so that Sheela would find the set-down bowl of sweets, would see September coming in first through the door and think that something had happened to July?

September could make her sister do anything. Had always been able to. The way September was with July sometimes reminded her of how Peter had been with her: his withholding of love for tactical advantage, the control concealed within silky folds of care. It wasn't the same, she thought over and over, September was not like that man. Except sometimes she wondered.

There were moments, particular ages, when the link between the two seemed to loosen and – in turn – they would soften individually as well, September's sharpness, July's anxious mania. Sheela thought that maybe these moments were brought on by the divisions their small age differences brought up. The time September lost her first tooth and July didn't; the moment September started her period and July lagged a couple of months behind, the words that September learned before July could speak. It was better then. She hated herself for thinking it but she liked when they weren't quite as inseparable, when there was more room for her. July would come and chat to her in the kitchen after dinner, September would sometimes read the picture books when she was working on them and give her notes. She considered again and again moving them to different schools, enforcing some sort of system of rules, finding a therapist who could see them separately, but she could never quite do it. Their bold happiness when they were close to one another, the protection they wound around each other like cotton wool. She hadn't had siblings and she wished, watching them, that she had.

The first time she drew them they were very young and she had done a couple of picture books before but nothing of any merit. Five, sometimes six days a week she worked at Blackwell's bookshop on the till and in her spare time she tried to find the idea for a book which would enable her to stop. She wrote in bed for lack of a desk and hid the drawings that were no good under the mattress.

The girls had been playing downstairs and had been quiet for longer than they should have been. She put her feet into her slippers and padded down to check on them. They had made some kind of den out of sofa cushions with coats draped over the back of chairs. July was inside, whispering something that sounded like a spell and September was on the sofa, arms raised.

I've got a torch, she yelled at Sheela as she came in. And this is a rope. OK?

OK, Sheela said and went back upstairs and drew them. The sofa was a cliff and the fort was a cave and they were there, somehow made understandable with pen and paper, made holdable.

By the time they were fifteen and sixteen they were close as they'd ever been. September answering every question for her sister, their meals carefully divided sharing platters, their heads close together on the same pillow. She had worried that things would go further, would spill over, that September's anger would get the better of her. And that was what had happened, wasn't it? Everything had built and built and built and then spilled over. The phone ringing through the dying-day house, tripping down the last step to get to it, the slight hesitation when she picked up and then the indrawn breath.

2

The first time they had come to the house September was just eleven and July was ten. The year before September had insisted – despite Sheela's protestations – on merging their birthdays and now the 5th of September was a day for both of them, two cakes, double presents, ribbons wound into their hair.

All year she hadn't been able to write, struggled to get out of bed. The doctor she went to see put her on medication that made it feel as if she was up to her waist in a marsh. She didn't want to hurt herself on the medication but she didn't want to do anything else either. She stopped taking the pills, cancelled the therapy sessions she had booked in, rang Ursa to check the house was free, packed the car. September kicked the back of her chair for the first half of the journey, demanded different radio stations. In Sheela's mind going to the house would feel like relief, everything falling away, the white walls a calmness, the bedroom soft and forgiving. She could not trust her own flesh but the house would cocoon them, would protect them all in a way she had become unable to do.

The first days were good and she was glad they had come. The weather was glorious and they spent as much time as they could outside, on the beach or in the sea, lying on blankets, eating sandwiches. The sea was cold and the sun was hot and she could feel her sunburn and the pain when September pulled her hair; she could feel the sadness at a dead seal they found and she laughed when July tripped and nearly went face first into a rock pool. July would fall asleep curled in her lap. September spoke to her about the birds she could see out at sea.

Except then, a day of storms, woken by rain, trapped in the house. Her face in the bathroom mirror like a double who wore her skin. The girls' voices grating on her, the words they said all somehow turned to harm. The walls seemed so close, they hemmed her in.

An awful Friday – she had to look up the day on her calendar – when nothing went right. She broke a mug in the kitchen and despair filled all the hollows and caves inside her. She could remember what it meant to be relieved and annoyed and pissed off and excited and tired from a long good day but, right now, she only felt dread. D-R-E-A-D. The word spelling out behind her eyes. A sound from somewhere in the house, a clatter and then a short, sharp exclamation immediately muffled. She left the broken mug where it lay and ran to them. There was blood on July's face and on her hands, the red like an alarm bell ringing in the deadening grey. Her questions were met with September's lined mouth and lidded eyes,

July's terrified, enforced silence. What had happened? Why had it? What were they thinking? The cut was superficial and the blood overly dramatic. She bandaged July and then took them to their room, gave them water and sat watching over them until September's scowls grew too much and she went back to bed, lay there with the door open listening to the sound of them moving around, laughing as if nothing had happened. What a day. What a day to be alive. She couldn't stand it. They could play there for a long time and not think of her or realise that they were on their own. She put on her shoes and coat at the door, took the car keys from the hook hammered into the wall.

The car stalled a few times up the hill but she eased it along, put on the windscreen wipers. She remembered a pub she had been to with Peter once, years ago. She drove instinctively. When she got there the car park was nearly full and she left the car jammed onto the verge.

The pub was busy but she did not let herself hesitate. There was a band, men in their fifties playing cover songs, families with children and a couple of tables of teenagers drinking spirits. She ordered a beer and found a quiet corner. Drank three in quick succession. There were other people around her drinking the way she was: with intent. There were dogs yipping and fighting in the middle of the room, rushing back to their owners and then out into the melee. Children joined them, screamed and were bitten and laughed and ran around wildly. She ordered some chips and ate them with ketchup. The band played faster songs, the words slurring together and lost.

Someone banged into her chair and she lost half her pint. As he was buying her another, apologising and grinning, she examined him. She could feel the dread at the bottom of her abdomen and in her chest; it felt like giving in. He had ancient hands, receding hair, a taut little beer belly, but his mouth was fat-lipped and sensual. He asked her questions and she told him everything he wanted to know. She felt a great exhaustion at his words and towards the taste of the beer and the clothes she was wearing and the children she had back at the house. He put his hand on her arm.

Another?

Not here, she said.

They drove in tandem, his headlights blinding her on the bumpy road. She coughed, opened the window to let the cold air blast her into clarity. They parked up outside the house. She held a finger to her lips and they tiptoed up the stairs like teenagers, rolling along the walls, silencing one another with hands to each other's mouths. She paused outside the girls' room, listening. It was quiet, they were sleeping.

In the bedroom they worked out how to get to one another and what to do about being so drunk. Maybe he hadn't been with anyone for a long time either. She could feel how much she wanted it even through the distance of the sadness. There was a song in her head that kept going around and round, certain words making plosive sounds in her thoughts, almost unbearable. She kept thinking of all the things that weren't sexy: doctors' appointments and giving birth in that same room and

104

the colour of the ambulance lights across the walls, chopping courgettes and the smell when you forget to hang out the laundry.

He was sucking on her nipples but they were so sensitive it hurt and she pushed him down. He went willingly and she looked at his unfamiliar head, working over her vulva, searching for her clit, and then he had it and she felt close immediately. The orgasm was both too good and too awful, the clenching of it. She didn't want to have intercourse afterwards so she lay on her back and he touched his nipples and she moved her hand up and down his penis until she saw his eyes going wide. As he was coming she thought she heard a noise and told him he had to leave and watched as he put on his clothes and went.

In the morning it might not have happened at all. The girls were in the garden, hanging from the washing line. She opened her arms and July came rushing over, hair swirling, barrelling into her. She held her. Over July's shoulder September was observing them carefully, one shoe tunnelling down into the mud. Sheela closed her eyes to shut her out.

July

1

The day after the night before, September says, and crushes me paracetamol, mixes the powder into milk, opens a tin of peaches and runs me a bath.

I don't remember how we got home, I say and tug at my dress, watch sand falling from the lining onto the sofa.

I carried you, you weigh a ton, September says.

In the bathroom she pulls my dress over my head. It smells like seaweed and blood. When she is stirring the bath, I look at the lining and there is a smear of rusty red. And, yes, I remember his hands then, on and not quite on me, his mouth there and not there. The bathroom floor hurts my knees, the sick in the toilet bowl is the colour of cider and meat. September tugs my hair away from my face, wipes the sweat off my forehead with the flat of her hand.

You've got some bruises, she says close to my face, leaning forward.

What?

She jabs down on the top of my chest and the pain brings another wave of sickness, my head ten times bigger than it should be. When I look down, I can see them, new and reddish-coloured, expansive. She prods at another and I say Ow and bat her away.

Fingerprints, I say, looking at the upside-down shape, and she lifts me up with her hands in my armpits and says, You must have bashed yourself, you drunkard. Get in.

The bath is hot and good and I sink in so that only my ears and mouth and nose are above the surface. September perches on the toilet seat and flashes hand signals at me that I don't understand. The water is tinged with red – the way it had been that day in the swimming pool – and there is pain, deep down and in my abdomen.

I could feel it, I say.

What do you mean? September pulls at a fingernail with her teeth.

I felt it happening.

She pulls her legs up onto the toilet seat. Cool.

It happened to me too, I say. Second-hand. It felt as if my hands and mouth were full and then there was some pain. Did you feel it?

It had felt momentous but she seems unfazed.

Maybe, she says.

Like magic, I say. We lost our virginity together. Like magic.

I drop down into the water so it surges over my face and try to remember exactly how it had felt, his tongue in my mouth, the cold air on my bare legs. I remember, also, the way he had moved close to me by the fire, touching my shoulder with his, his mouth against my cheek. He had wanted me. Could that be right? Yes, he had wanted me and then September lifting her dress over her head, pulling him away.

You had sex with him even though you knew I liked him.

I hadn't thought I'd said the words out loud but she swivels to stare at me, her face flat and blank as a reptile's, her hands raised. She shrugs.

You weren't ever going to do anything about it. I helped you.

I wish I hadn't spoken, that I could draw the words back into my mouth. She is angry with me and I am uncertain what she will do with the anger.

You could text him a photo, she says and the words are so nasty that I feel them physically like stones.

My hangover gets worse, bearing down on the top of my head. September says my skin is clammy and drags the duvet down the stairs and wraps me up on the sofa and brings me hot water to sip from. I keep thinking about what happened on the beach and sometimes I see it through September's eyes and sometimes through my own, the water-sodden dress and the grit of sand. I doze in and out of consciousness, my mouth beach-dry, my eyelids glued together. When I open my eyes I see September is there, standing over me, watching, her mouth filled with teeth and her eyes filled with the reflection of me on the sofa.

Later I drink from the tap with my hands, glugging up the water, trailing the duvet behind me. September is not on the sofa or in the bathroom or the pantry or the kitchen. I go upstairs in search of her. Not in our bedroom or the airing cupboard.

I lay my head against Mum's door. Silence. I would not dare but September would and so I do. I put my hand on the doorknob and turn it slowly, push the door inwards and then sidle inside. The room smells musty and there are piles of smeary plates and grubby mugs on the floor, glasses of water littering all the surfaces. Mum is in bed with the duvet pulled nearly over her head, facing away from me. I watch her ribs rise and fall. I think of her coming down in the night so that she won't run into us, moving around without turning the lights on, her tired face lit by the glow from the fridge.

There is a desk in the corner of the room. I go over and grip the back of the chair, stand looking down at the drawings laid out. The drawings in the rest of her picture books are brightly coloured and all outside, on clifftops or in forests, the two of us running along the top of a wall or walking crouched through dim caves. These are different. They are all of the Settle House. A few are of the sitting room from various angles: September curled on the sofa asleep or stood in front of the television or plaiting her own hair; in one she is changing the light bulb in the pantry. The rooms in the pictures look small and shadowy. I move a couple aside. September cuts slivers from a cheese block on the counter; she carries boxes up the stairs or reads or moves the magnetic letters around on the fridge. September peers around the pantry door, climbs down the ladder from the top bunk bed. I shuffle through them again. I am not in a single drawing. One slips from the pile and onto the floor and I bend to pick it up. It is a drawing of the bathroom, September is in the bath with wet hair, her knees drawn up to her chin. There is something different about it. I hold it close to my face in the low light. There is a slip of silver in the mirror, the beginnings of what might be a hand, emerging out from the surface of the reflection.

Mum sits up in the bed. I freeze. She rubs her eyes with her fists, her hair is matted. I slide towards the door.

September? she says.

I am nearly out. If she turned her head, she would see me. I almost go to her. If she said my name, I would go to her. She is still half asleep, dreaming perhaps. I put my hand on the doorknob and turn it.

When I go back downstairs September rises from the sofa, limbs as long as tree branches, wide-faced, the bones of her taking up more room than I ever remember them taking up. She cuts me chunks of bread but wrinkles her nose when I try to offer her some. She turns on the TV and watches it upside down, her head hung off the bottom of the sofa. I want to tell her about the pictures but I won't. In Mum's books September has always been the fierce one. When we were ten I was kidnapped by a minotaur and September rescued me from the maze. When I was twelve I fell into a water tank and September had to work out how to get me out before the water rose to the top. When I was fourteen I read the wrong instructions in an ancient book and September had to stop the end of the world from happening. But I was always in the pictures, even if somewhere off to the side.

She has unearthed the binoculars and is carrying them around her neck, now and then lifting them up to peer into the eyeglass.

Let's go, she says. I'm bored. I'm fucking bored.

Where? I can hear a whine in my voice.

I don't know. To the beach.

She has that look in her eyes and I don't dare say that I don't want to. We put on boots. The air is hot on our exposed faces after the cool of the house. The sun has burnt the clouds away and the earth is breaking, the grass browning.

September pulls me along faster. We are heading to the beach on the same path we'd gone along the day before. I know I will see it and then I do. The bird-watching hut ahead of us, the drop of darkness beneath, the grass growing in some places almost all the way up to the narrow viewing window which runs like a pursed mouth around the sides.

I can hear myself mewling but September's grip is strong on my hand. The birdwatching box is all I can see; it obliterates the horizon. I imagine what it will be like inside, the walls closing in, the smell of damp, the hustle of rain on the roof although it is not raining.

I thought we were going to the beach, I say.

Don't be a party-pooper.

The shadow of the box falls onto us. My skin feels cinched in at the back and the neck, between the fingers. September wraps her arm around my waist and bears me forward, my feet skidding across the ground. The steps are green with growth; we stumble up them.

Come on, come on.

There is a sign on the door which I had not seen before: the bird box is out of use and trespassing is forbidden. My stomach cramps. September bashes inside. There are old cans of Stella on the floor, a scattering of cigarette butts, a condom packet. The smell of rotting, softening wood, of roots and vegetation. I put my hands on my knees and the dizziness swarms, seeps, retreats. September is cavorting around, kicking at the cans. She steers me towards a bench and pushes me down, pulls the binoculars from around my neck where I do not remember putting them, holds them up in front of my face and aims them at the gap in the side of the hut.

What do you see?

I don't answer and she groans, takes the binoculars off me.

The tide is out, she says, there are some birds on the beach looking for worms or little crabs. There's something black diving into the water and it's got a fish, I think.

I get very cold. September says my lips are blue and she puts my fingers into her mouth and sucks them to try and warm them up but somehow they come out colder than when they went in. Something is happening. The beach turns chalky. I think about our dad coming here, wrapped up with a Thermos or a couple of sandwiches, sitting for a very long time.

Dusk makes the sky thick and creamy, coffee-coloured, and with it comes a new beginning. September lets in a sharp breath and leans forward. The space around my eyes hurts and my vision is blurred with shuddering shapes, blackening the air.

There's something there, she says. She lifts the binoculars to my eyes, forcing me to look out.

The birds are tiny but they have massed together into a multitude and are rising and falling and etching across the sky, now dropping and now shivering up again, waves, before diving down into the thick reeds. Even from inside the hut I can hear the sound of their wings. Another group comes, bigger than the first, and drops into the reeds just as a third group – from a different direction – takes its place, roiling across the diminishing sky, calling to itself, bubbling up and around, falling into the grass and then suckering up once more. There is something black and monstrous moving through the stalks, rushing back and forth, making a catastrophe of noise. And then I understand that it is the birds, drawn so close together they seem like a single animal, crashing among the foliage, trying to find somewhere to come to rest.

I can feel the hot tears on my face. I get up. I do not look back though I know that September is standing at the door of the hut, watching me go. I skid on the sand and nearly go down. There is the sound of rain although the night is clear, the star crusts of spume across the sky, the eddying of the sea not far off, the roof of the house emerging like folded arms from the slope. I can feel the pull of September, calling me back to her. The boom of unspilled blood battling through me, the door of the house like relief in front of me, the sudden silence as I move inside.

I lie almost sleeping waiting for the sound of September coming home. I imagine her out in the night, rushing between the reeds like a multiple-bodied creature, down to the waves and digging into the sand with her thousand heads and wings. The weight of her on the bed, the feel of her hand smoothing my hair.

Later, in the bathroom, sleep clinging, my period has come. I fumble at the tampon wrapper, do it wrong, have to open another. The blood on the toilet roll is different to the way it normally is, brown and clotted and my ribs look like the bellows of the accordion someone once played in assembly at school. Flushing the chain I see that there is something on my lower left arm, the size of a pound coin. I rub at it, lick my finger, rub. It doesn't come off. The skin is crinkled, off-white. I run it under the tap but it stays the same.

2

Mum always says we are too old for hide-and-seek but we don't care. September is best at it. I stay in the kitchen and count, listen to the sound of her thumping away, dodging back and forward the way she always does so I can't tell where her footsteps are leading. Her favourite game is to play hide-and-seek in the snow, leaving her footprints for me to see but sometimes stepping back into them to hide the way or making fake prints with her hands or covering them over entirely so I never quite know where she has gone. I count to a hundred. Ready or not.

There are a few obvious places which I check first. Behind the sofa, tucked into the fireplace nook, in the bath, behind the stairs with the bookcases. She is in none of the places I look; she is too good for them. She isn't in the pantry either. The light is still broken but I stand holding the door open and listening for a long time, peering in at the shelves.

I go up and down the main stairs a few times to put her off. In our game of hide-and-seek you can move as many times as you want, sneaking from place to place, going somewhere the hunter has already looked. She often favours small spaces – almost too small for her to fit into – underneath beds or wedged into cupboards. In the bedroom I walk on tiptoe, nudging the door open, almost entirely silent. If you catch a person unawares the reward is greater. Something makes a sound like a glass bottle rolling on a wooden floor outside in the corridor and I rush towards it, arms wide: got you. Except she is not there. Nothing is there.

I have given away my position so I move quickly, noisily now, stamping my feet in an exaggerated way on the floor. In the bedroom we sleep in someone has tidied up. Not me or September, Mum then. The clothes we'd strewn around the room and on the bottom bed before the beach party are folded, laid out in single piles on the floor, tights and underwear balled on top of each pile, a full outfit. As if a person has just wriggled out of them. The duvet on the bottom bunk bed looks rounded, fuller than it should. I pretend to open the cupboard and look between the hangers, clattering them loudly, and then move to the bed in three long steps, waving my arms for balance.

I think I see soles of feet flashing beneath the duvet. Tear it back, an Aha on my tongue, almost out of my mouth, swallowed. The bed is empty. I climb onto the top bunk but that is empty too.

I chuck the duvet onto the floor, go back out into the corridor. I am afraid and for a moment – less than a moment – I imagine that my body is September's body and brace my legs against either side of the corridor, put my hands on my hips, listen. A noisy house. Creaking and hissing, the boiler, water dripping somewhere, the sound of the fan whirring in the bathroom. I open the door to the airing cupboard, step quietly inside and close the door, crouch down.

I accidently brush my arm against the hot boiler and kick out my feet into the wall in front of me. It gives beneath my flailing heels, falling inward: a wall that is not a wall. I peer through the gap. There is a space beyond, between the inner and outer walls of the house, a narrow alleyway with just space to fit through. A perfect hiding place. Clever September. I will not be afraid now; I will find her and she will be pleased with me.

I clamber into the space, replace the fallen board behind me, stand up and begin to move along, tucking my elbows in, suppressing coughs with the flat of my hand. I can see – there is light from the airing cupboard behind me and seemingly coming through the walls – footprints in the grimy floor, clean marks, each toe clearly picked out: a trail. I put my feet inside each print and they fit perfectly. I listen and it is true that something might be moving away in front of me, around the curve of the wall, an indrawn breath, the sound of laughter withheld. I think how much I love her and put my hands over my mouth to stop my own laughter, go faster, smudging the prints with my feet.

Just beyond where I am stood there is a scattering of things on the floor which I bend down to pick up. Dead ants, ancient, desiccated. I put them in my pocket.

The rattle of fast-moving feet nearing me, thundering – I straighten – coming towards me around the bend, getting closer. I hold my arms out to reach for her, close my eyes, whistle a rising scale for her the way she would do for me, a celebration song. I do not think to be afraid, not then, not in that moment. There is silence. I open my eyes. There is no one there. I wriggle around the corner to look down the next side of the wall space but it is empty. There are not – I see looking down – even footprints in the dust. And then I am fear-filled, stumbling away, knocking into the partition, bending to squeeze through, all elbows and knees, all July and none of September's bare-faced, rock-laughing bravery in me.

September is standing in the hallway, hands on her hips, eyeing me. I look at her feet to see if they are dirty but the black socks she is wearing are clean.

You are rubbish at this game, she says. Shall we watch something?

We slump together on the sofa, September's hot, slightly metallic breath on my cheek. I touch her fingers and shoulder, stroke the side of her face. She tugs away, makes a humming noise at the programme on the TV. A nature programme we've watched so many times I could narrate it with my eyes closed. I straighten up.

How did you do that behind the walls? I say.

Huh?

Are you listening?

She nods against my shoulder.

How did you get out of the wall so fast?

She raises her head and looks at me, her eyes narrowed so that the pupils are only thin slivers. Get out of the wall? Don't be silly, July.

You know what I mean. Through the airing cupboard, the loose board. That's where you were hiding.

No, it wasn't.

Yes, it was. I heard you and then you were gone. I was scared.

She blinks at me. The TV turns her skin to marshland. She wets her lips with her tongue. That wasn't where I was hiding, July-bug. You found me; don't you remember? I was in bed. It wasn't a very good hiding place. It's not a good hide-and-seek house. Maybe we could play on the dunes next time.

I look at her face and she looks back, unblinking. I can see the beginning of an argument coming, the line of stubbornness which says she won't back down, that I will have to. I've never been good at lying but that is not something you could say about September. When we were children she would make me promise not to tell but I would always give it away. Did you take the coins from the side? Mum would say. Did you set fire to this toilet roll? Did you bury the end of the washing line? No, I'd say but my neck would go hot-blotchy and I'd start stuttering. One of the teachers had taken me aside once and said, Does September make you do things you don't want to do? And I'd said no no no no but underneath the no there was a maybe that I only think about at times like this.

120

I remember, you're right. I had a dream and got confused.

She smiles at me and turns my head so she can knot my hair into tufts which stick up from my scalp.

September goes to bed but I can't sleep. The house is different at night. I don't turn on any of the lights and keep accidently walking into walls, rebounding off furniture. Nothing, I'm certain, is in the place it was during the day. My eyes acclimatise gradually, I start to see the shapes of things. There is the sofa, there are the bookshelves, there is the door into the pantry or the kitchen.

I drink four glasses of water as fast as I possibly can. I look in all the pockets of the coats hanging up by the front door and find three loose buttons, a smattering of change, rolled-up tissues, dog biscuits. I arrange them on the floor in concentric circles and then put everything in the fridge in size order, largest to smallest. The light from the fridge shows parts of the room around me, everything shadowy and dim, and I think sometimes that there is motion in the parts I can't see well enough. My eyes hurt and I close the fridge and crawl along the floor, facing upwards, my elbows bent back, like a crab. I lean against the wall and push my legs up and stay there, upside down, as long as I can, until all the blood rushes to my head.

I go to the bathroom. Mum's been cleaning when we aren't around and there is the smell of bleach, although the corners of the room are grimy and the taps are clogged around the base with limescale, the plughole in the bath matted with something wiry and coiled. I flush the toilet and stand in front of the mirror. I stare at myself, waiting for something to happen, and then, slowly, it does. I look more like September than I have ever done before. The shape of my face is the shape of her face, my eyes are lightened and narrowed, the look in them so like the look that is often in hers. She gazes out of my coating, like a thief caught breaking into a building. In the mirror I can see that the mark on my arm has spread, stretching now nearly down to the wrist and up to the crease in the elbow. September wears me like a coat.

I go into the kitchen and rifle through the drawer. The wind suckers at the corners of the window and I find the right sort, thin at the tip.

Back in the bathroom. The mark is crinkled, the skin rucked like messy plaster. I measure it with my thumb. I line the knife up and dig at the place on my forearm. A bit of the skin comes away. There is a ringing in my ears. I push the next bit up, wedging the knife in, the soft skin beneath like curd, and a lot comes up in a sheet, sticky, clinging to the flesh beneath which is yellowing, bad-looking, bad-smelling, the surface marred with lines and softening spots, the flesh turned white in places, the hair coming away with the skin. There is no pain and then there is. I can hear someone shouting something, they are shouting: What are you doing? September, what are you –

3

In the morning September presents me with paint and brushes and says we're going to paint the sitting room. She seems buoyed by the idea, full of energy. She puts on some music and dances, arms in the air, shunting her hips back and forth. I dance too and she laughs at me and says I look like an old dad doing the Macarena so I stop.

Fine, I say, I'll move the furniture all on my own. Except I don't really mind.

I heave the sofa into the middle of the room and drag the TV away from the wall, move the empty shelves. Behind the furniture the walls are peely with paint, the plaster loose and crumbly. We scrape a lot of it away with spoons and the wallpaper stripper. September wraps a scarf around my face to keep out the worst of it but, still, I have to stop often and rest, go into the bathroom to spit up powdery phlegm. There is a strange array of colours in the paint pots, none of them quite right.

Mum doesn't like red, September says.

She does, what about that dress?

She only wore that once.

Well. She definitely doesn't like blue.

You don't know.

I do.

In the end we get a saucepan from the kitchen and mix together a few different colours, aiming for purple and almost getting there. We rest and I eat some bread and cheese Mum must have left out. I try to get September to eat some, making a game out of it, whizzing the bread through the air towards her mouth but she only crinkles her nose and glares until I stop.

In the night I'd wrapped my arm up in a bandage and taped down the corners. I keep waiting for September to notice and ask what happened but if she sees it she doesn't say anything. I go to the bathroom and pretend to wee with the tap running and search my body for other marks, odd spots, things that weren't there before. I scratch the side of the bandage off expecting to see the softening crust, the unhealed flesh, but the mark has grown back in the night and worse, the skin thick, flaking away a little. There is a new mark, also, on the top of my thigh, bigger than the first. I push my trousers down and squeeze it between my fingers. The skin is dry like baking paper and rough, bubbled like the odd wallpaper in the old house in Oxford. I squeeze and squeeze, trying to force the colour out, like a spot, but the mark stays the same. I wrap my hands as far around my thighs as they can go, certain I've shrunk again in the night. September starts yelling my name, saying fuck after each word, and I yank my trousers up and go into the sitting room.

Come on, she says, let's do this.

We load paint onto the brushes and coat the wall with it, moving our arms rhythmically up and down, covering as much space as we can. It is not entirely successful. The loose plaster coats the brushes – makes them claggy – and the paint fills the holes but looks uneven, rough and ragged. We plough on regardless; it is too late to retreat now. I get a big smear across my face and feel ridiculous, paint in my mouth and nose. September does the same to make me feel better, rubbing the brush into her hair, across her eyelids.

I look at the walls. She'll like it, I say.

She will.

We move around the room. It is harder work than I'd supposed and my arms ache, my lungs burn. I rest, sprawling on the sofa, getting paint on the cushions by accident. September keeps working, sloshing the paint onto the wall, rubbing her fingers into it.

Time does an odd thing, goes backwards and forwards, making my head spin. I look up and we've hardly painted any of the wall, just a thin slice; I resurface and the entire wall is done and September is closing the bathroom door, everything slowed to a trickle so that hours, perhaps days, are spent watching her face thinning in the gap, there, there, nearly gone, gone. I come back and September is working quickly, speeding across the wall, paintbrush jerking, the paint on me dried into a painful layer.

I'm hungry, I say and she stops and finds me a crumpet, toasts it, spreads it with butter; I eat it quickly, desperate for the next one.

We finish the first coat and then, without pausing, start going around and doing the second.

Maybe we should have waited for it to dry, I say when we've been working for ten minutes or so but September only grunts and keeps going.

The paint is sticky and the paintbrushes are matted. We labour on without a break and finish as it is getting dark. The muscles in my arms throb.

When I look around the lamps are on and September isn't there. My shadow has moved across the room with me and now stands almost in line, as if holding my feet with her hands. The walls are dark purple. I open my mouth to shout September's name and then close it again. Don't caterwaul at me, she'll say, I'll come when I want to. The room looks smaller than it was before, as if we've painted ourselves into a cave.

There is a spot, beside the window, that looks particularly wet, sagging a little. I step closer, reach out, touch the wall with my index finger and it gives, soggy, my finger passing all the way through and into the cold space beyond. I pull my finger out. There is a sound coming from inside the wall, the rustle and gurgle of motion, the shuttering of thousands of wings. I put my ear to the hole and listen. It is the sound the birds made as they fell down towards the earth, rushed through the reeds.

The side of my face itches. I slap my hand against my cheek. An ant. I look at it and then at the wall. There are ants pouring out. They get stuck in the paint and are trapped, wriggling, straining away to try and pull themselves free. The ones that come after climb over the trapped insects, using them to clamber away; there are lots, too many to count. They come out in a rush and the softened wall gives, the hole widening against their small, tough forms. Something is screaming in the wall. There is a flurry at the entrance and a beak appears, tearing at the plaster, the small black body out and the wings caught behind. I touch it, the burring, vibrating warmth of feathers, the flurrying anguished pulse.

The ants swarm over the bird, burying themselves in it, covering it, digging beneath the down and I open my mouth to shout and shout.

It is very late and very dark, and I am in the bedroom although I do not know how I got there. I am flat on my back and September is crouched on top of me, knees tucked either side of my waist, forehead nearly touching mine. Her eyes are closed. I move a little and her knees constrict against my torso, her hands bear down onto my chest, flattened, the fingers gouging in. I open my mouth to shout at her and she draws in a big breath and any words I was about to say are sucked from me and into her.

What a dream, I think, what a dream and then it is the morning and I am standing in front of the place where I'd pushed my finger through the wall. It is possible, I think, that I have been there all night. There is no hole. I run my hand over the surface, checking. The paint has dried in globules and unattractive runnels but the wall is solid.

4

In the Settle House the fitful nights murmur, sleep like blankets piled on top of my head, exhausted through the long, long days hemming always into darkness. Waking coughing; having to stop at the top of the stairs to catch my breath, feeling sick unless I'm eating and then feeling desperate, shovelling it in, whatever I can find. Two weeks in the Settle House. Two weeks in the house where September was born and where she – at least – seems at home, freezing as if listening to words I can't hear, wandering off without saying anything and reappearing hours later, bright-eyed, sidelong grin. Sometimes a thought rising up from the tiredness, from the hunger, barely there, already almost submerged: something had happened that day at the tennis courts. Something had happened we could not remember.

The Settle House is load-bearing. Here is what it bears: Mum's endless sadness, September's fitful wrath, my quiet failures to ever do quite what anyone needs me to do, the seasons, the death of small animals in the scrub-lands around it, every word that we say in love or anger to one another.

I do not remember the tennis courts but I remember something else. We are eleven and ten and we are playing September Says in the dark Settle House. It is day but we have drawn the curtains and thrown cardigans over the lamps so that the light is tinged with colours, blues and greens, an orange pool near the window. Mum had come down and made pizza for dinner and the smell of burnt dough lingers. September had fought with her and Mum had retreated once more. September's eyes are narrowed. I placate her with everything I do.

September says do the robot.

I twist my body mechanically and pivot my arm stiffly in its socket and September claps.

September says kiss your hand.

I smother my hand with my mouth, lick my fingers, hold my lips to my palm until she laughs and I feel a wave of satisfaction at the sound.

Move, she says and I freeze. Light yourself on fire. I stand very still. Break your own arm. I don't move. Scream until you are blind. I don't even blink.

September says do the flamenco, she says and I parade around the room, flicking my feet up, twirling my hands, throwing my plait around my head.

September says eat all the mayonnaise, she says and I groan but get the jar from the fridge and sit on the sofa with a teaspoon. September watches me, occasionally helping out with a spoon or two, cheering when I seem to be flagging. My tummy aches but I finish the whole jar and then hold it above my head while she whoops. We hear Mum coming down the stairs and scuttle into the bathroom. I listen with my ear to the wood, waiting to see if she'll go back upstairs. There is the sound of her moving around the kitchen.

September says run your hand under the hot tap for a minute, she says from behind me. I turn to check she is serious but she is examining her face in the mirror, pulling at the skin on her cheeks, prodding her neck. I turn the hot tap on and hold my hand beneath it, count out loud. I can see her eyes flicking down to check I am doing it right. The tap takes a long time to get warm but by the end of the minute the water is very hot. My hand is red. September sucks my fingers and pats my head and pulls herself up to sit on the side of the sink. I try to think of a reason to end the game, to find a way out, but she is too fast for me.

September says hold your breath for a minute, she says and counts for me while I bulge my cheeks and screw my eyes shut.

September says slap me, she says and I pull my hand back and then bring it lightly against her face, hardly making a sound. Her look is disgusted. One life gone. September says SLAP ME, and I pull my hand back again and bring it forward against her cheek which turns instantly red while she howls and then cackles until I too start laughing and barely hear what she has said.

What?

131

She repeats it, watching me.

September says cut yourself here. She points to the bottom of her neck. September says do it now or lose the whole game. September says hurry up.

I think for a moment maybe I won't and then I know that I will. The air is concrete. Mum is banging around upstairs but she will not come in time. The game has never gone this way before although it has always threatened to: September says swallow this tiny battery, go lie in the road when the lights are red.

I can only just reach but I open the medicine cabinet and take out the pack of razors Mum keeps there to shave her legs. Their heads are bristling with her dark hair. I take one out and draw it quickly across the top of my chest. Nothing happens. I do it again, sideways this time, and the pain is sharp and quick and I feel the hot wet and make a sound which must penetrate out and into the kitchen and then Mum is there, taking it in, reaching out and perhaps this time, anyway, I will tell her and there will be a breaking between September and me, it will never be the same again. But she is fussing, asking ten questions a minute, and dragging out bandages from the cabinet and I do not tell her what happened. September is holding me and I do not tell her.

The days are threaded together with blood, sewn with the needle of red: the blood in the bathroom that day, the blood on the beach, the blood in the swimming pool. I jerk at the mark on my arm, wanting to see beneath, but it won't give. There is a patch on my stomach today glazed like sugar. I think of showing September but she is in a bad mood again, stomping around, shoving furniture out of place, changing the time on the clock so it reads wrong. The purpose with which we'd rushed around painting yesterday is gone. I tail her, knocking into her heels, nearly tripping her over.

Give it a rest, she hisses, leave me be.

I drop back but not all the way. Her anger is like a tide, tugging me in towards it. Her hair is dirty, clods of mud in the blonde, bits of what look like burnt paper scattering her shoulders. The day is properly hot, the house stagnant. I find ice creams that Mum must have bought in the freezer. Unwrap two and hold one out to her and she stares at me as if I'm mad. I wrap my tongue around mine and it cools the itch on my skin.

It's really good, I say and she knocks the one I offered to her out of my grip so that it falls to the floor and starts melting onto the tiles. I hold on to the stick of mine and it cuts into my hand and I think about what my skin has been doing, turning rough, and how if it kept going like this I would solidify entirely.

Are you OK? I say. Her eyes are so bright it almost hurts to look at them. September?

I knew about the photo, she says and she has the look on her face that I know means she wants to hurt me, will say whatever she can to do it. I didn't need to see the phone; I knew what you were doing. I saw the messages he sent you and I knew it wasn't him. Of course it wasn't him. Silly July-bug.

The ice cream is melting onto my hand, shockingly cold. She doesn't seem to be looking at me but, somehow, through me to the door behind.

It should have been you, she says but before I can respond someone rattles the letter box and then knocks on the door with both fists. There is the sound of movement on the loose-stoned drive, stumbling, someone knocking into the broken pots. A shadow falling through the window and across the dirty carpet. I drop to the floor, crouch beside September.

They have their face against the mucky window, hands cupped around their eyes to see. They say my name and I look back to September but she has gone, spirited away upstairs. I can just about see who it is, the red hair, the awkward slope of the shoulders.

I go to open the door and somewhere in the house September whistles a warning tune but doesn't come after me.

John looks a little sheepish, bare-armed. Hello, I thought I'd come by, he says.

He doesn't look much the way he does in my memory. I try to recall what it had been like to have almost sex with him but the recollection doesn't feel quite real. He smiles at me very wide.

I just wanted to see you, he says. I brought this. He holds up a bottle. Do you want some?

His body is as distracting as a flashing road sign and I can't remember what things people are supposed to say to one another. I wish that September would come and take control of the situation. She would be

134

dismissive or she would decide it was good he was there and she would be friendly and know exactly what to say. I wish this and at the same time I hope that she doesn't come back.

Is your mum here? he says. He has been out in the sun and his pale skin is burnt and peeling at the neckline. There are scoops of sweat beneath his arms.

My sister is upstairs. September is upstairs.

I look for a reaction to this news but he seems uninterested, raising the bottle and drinking from it. I can hear September moving around above us, pacing from one room to the other the way Mum had done in Oxford, after the fight at the school.

September is here, I say again.

OK, he says, widening his eyes at me.

Shall I go get her?

He doesn't answer.

He moves further into the house and examines it, pointing out things, the beams in the ceiling, the size and shape of the windows. We sit on the sofa and drink from the bottle. He talks openly and quickly without much need for me to say anything. He talks about his brothers who are all older and who crash every car they ever have and he talks about a few girls he is seeing at school, nothing serious, just this and that. As he speaks about the girls I see him looking sideways at me and I understand that he is asking what September would think about that, about him seeing other girls. I am embarrassed again and wish she would come downstairs and I am angry with her and at him. I take the bottle and drink, it burns a little as it goes down and I cough. When I stop, he's got his hand on my knee.

My sister's not here, I say. She's upstairs.

That's good.

He puts his face close to mine the way he'd done on the beach, his mouth against my cheek. His hand is on my knee and I am uncertain, because September is upstairs not here and I'd liked him before her, this strange, red-headed boy. I had liked him first and she had known about the photo and hadn't stopped me. I'm going to do this, I think. And I know that I am doing it to hurt her in the way that she sometimes does things to hurt me, and I think about how my face in the mirror had looked almost like hers.

I put my hand on his knee too and he seems to take this as invitation, his mouth moving to cover mine so that I taste his breath – the cigarette he must have smoked walking to the house, the bacon he'd had for breakfast – and wonder if it is the way it had tasted for September. The kissing goes on for a while but he seems unable or unwilling or too nervous to go further. I remember the second-hand feeling of what had happened before and reach towards him. It is like following a map. He leads me with the noises he makes which I find off-putting and awkward but which are helpful too. He moves fast towards some sort of conclusion that I am unsettled by. It seems better to linger and I remember it had been the same on the beach, a rush towards the end. It had felt historic the first time and it had not even really happened to me. This time it didn't really feel like anything.

That was just as good, he says when it is over. He has an arm flung around my shoulder so that my neck is in an uncomfortable position. I can feel him deflating. That was just as good as last time. He seems surprised and pleased and it's strange him comparing the two of us. It seems – though I don't know that I have enough knowledge of the matter to judge – not right to compare sisters. Last time you were good like that, he says, and I realise that he has confused us. We do not look the same at all, but he has confused us.

I lie very still worrying that he will discover his mistake and be angry, as if I were somehow complicit in the deception. He swigs the last inch of the bottle and starts talking again about his family and the farm they own, which he doesn't want to have anything to do with when he grows up.

I become aware of something in the house. A tensing; as of a gullet closing off oxygen. John does not seem to notice, he keeps talking, occasionally touching me with light, patting motions. The windows in the house shudder a little and I feel the walls draw in. There is the smell of burnt rubber and of a long rain left to sit and moulder on the ground. His hair sizzles with static and mine does too.

There is something different in his look when he eyes me and, trying to work it out, I realise that he is afraid. He clears his throat and moves to the other end of the sofa, sitting and mechanically putting one leg up onto the knee of the other. Not knowing what to do, I sit on the floor beside the fireplace. He starts talking in the way he had done before, rambling distractedly about his family and the cars they own and the dogs. Above us September crashes around. I can feel her anger even from here, the heat of it pooling at the top of my spine. John's voice drones on, his hands opening and closing in his lap. The words mean nothing to me. I think about that day at school. It seems that everything has been moving towards thinking about it. There is quiet from above and when I look towards the stairs September is there, squatting on the top step, looking down through the banisters at us.

My sister is here, I say to John.

He hesitates, looking at me and then around the room. OK, he says. I can meet her. If you want. He seems subdued, somehow shrunken. Any bravado he'd had when he came in has gone. I'd like to meet her, he says.

You have met her. I feel annoyed at him, at his latent stupidity, this ridiculous charade. You have met her, I say loud and his shoulders draw up towards his chin. On the beach. You met us both. Don't you remember?

He shakes his head, stands up, I don't know what you're talking about.

I feel disgusted by him. This game he is playing. I look to the top of the stairs to ask September to come down, to show herself so that there can be an end to it. John has moved close to the door and is rushing to put on his shoes. I look for her but September is already off the bottom of the stairs and is coming towards me. Her lips are moving but the words she says do not come from her but from the walls. They boom around the room, fill my ears so that I cannot hear my own thoughts, cannot make out any sound but September's voice. She is holding the binoculars. John is struggling with his shoes, hopping on one foot, his face reddening from the collar up. September is holding the binoculars and swinging them and her face is a face I know. She is holding the binoculars and moving them through the air and then I am holding them and they connect with the side of John's face and he seems stunned but fine for a moment and then is falling backwards onto the floor. He lies still.

5

There is a bruise coming already on John's forehead, tinting the skin. I am holding the binoculars in one hand and September is gone. The sitting room is empty around me. I am shaking. I bend down and touch John on the face. He is breathing but he does not wake up.

I go upstairs, calling September's name. The house is hot again, the radiators burning from the walls, the pipes banging over and over. I look for her in our room and, quietly, in the room Mum sleeps in. She is nowhere. I look for her beneath the beds and in the wardrobes. She will come out. She is making a joke. I know what she looks like when she laughs, her lips lifted into a snarl, the buttery texture of her gums.

I go back downstairs. John is not moving, and I wonder if I have killed him. I look in the pantry and then in the bathroom. There is the pop from somewhere above me of trees breaking in a storm and when I touch my head my hair is wet, I am soaking as if I have been

out in rain and my hands smell like smoke and burning.
The bottom of the bathtub is thick with leaves and dirt.
I open my mouth to shout September's name but nothing
comes out.

6

Storm Regina had come in the night, washed in on the torrent of rain. Someone said that the whole of Abingdon Road was flooded and people were going out in kayaks and paddling up and down, taking photos in front of the road sign to show they'd been there. Someone's child had drowned, fallen from a canal boat and been swept away. The drive to school took double the time it normally did; half the buses had stopped running and, once we arrived, a few of the classrooms were leaking and couldn't be used.

We rushed to and from class with our coats over our heads and our bodies soaked as soon as we left the building. Earlier in the week there had been sodden photos of me on the ground outside, all the ink running into the puddles, but they were gone now.

September and Kirsty had both been suspended from school for three days and when September came back she was stony-faced with her plan. When she spoke her words were sharp. She kept cutting across me, telling the servers at lunch what I wanted, answering for me in class. She carried my bag slung across the opposite shoulder from her own, sometimes leaned towards me as I was working and changed the answers so that her handwriting became imposed on mine.

She had told Lily and the others to meet us at the tennis courts after school. I do not know how the conversation had gone or what they thought she wanted to do there. That morning she had slid the knife into her pocket. Next to her in class or in the toilet at break or at lunch eating mashed potato and cheese I kept thinking I'd tell her that I didn't want us to do it, that we were going to call it off. At lunch in the hall I imagined how authoritative my voice would be, how I would bring my fist down on the table for emphasis, how she would look annoyed and then accepting and how, afterwards, our relationship would be ever so slightly changed, how she would listen to me and listen when I said I didn't want to do something, how we would finally be equal. Looking up I see Ryan watching us from across the room, his arms folded on the table, furrows between his eyes.

What is it? September said, turning her gaze furiously onto the room.

Nothing, I said but I thought – before I could stop myself – what it would be like if it was just me, if I had been born first and then September hadn't come at all. I would have friends, perhaps, and Ryan might ask me a question in class and then laugh at my answer or we'd walk around the field together or he'd touch my shoulder or he'd –

Come on, we're finished, September said and pushed my food onto her tray to take to the bin. I felt suddenly guilty, wrapped my arms around her middle and she kissed my forehead.

The storm was bad and some of the others went home at lunchtime but we did not. September was lit up from the inside out, her white smile and pale hair, the words falling over one another to get out of her. I remember every small moment. How she bent over the water fountain and came up wiping her mouth on the back of her sleeve. How she made me play hangman over and over, the small man building himself across the page. What words did she choose? S-W-A-L-L-O-W, C-A-V-I-N-G, B-U-R-I-E-D. She kept checking the clock and I kept looking at her face as she did it and watching the expressions that passed over her, the excitement and the nerves.

After lunch she had maths and I had sports. The changing rooms were leaking and chilly. I watched my skin turning porridge-like. The teacher was bored, on her phone, and we did suicide runs up and down, bending to tap the white line and then turning to run the other way. Ryan was there. I hadn't noticed and then I saw him flashing past, the arc of his skinny arms held up beside his chest, the blur of his bony knees beneath the shorts. The teacher blew her whistle and we all gathered up, puffing, hands on our thighs. He was next to me. I looked down at his scuffed trainers on the floor, his breath steadying, the wipe of sweat on his neck.

Hey, he said. I knew that he was speaking quietly so that no one else could see that he was talking to me. I didn't answer.

I wanted to say sorry, he said. That it happened. I wanted to say sorry.

There was a hole in the roof somewhere and water was coming through and splashing, gathering into a puddle. The air smelled stale, like feet and sweat. I could smell him, I think, the undertone of his deodorant. I could have said something then, formed some sentence which would have drawn us together, but the teacher was yelling at us to get up and the storm sounded closer than it had done before and he just smiled a bit and kicked his legs out and jogged back to the white line.

September was waiting for me in the corridor outside the changing rooms. The rain was hammering down, unhesitating, great slips and streams of it crashing from the gutters. I could see that already she was considering what was to come, she was barely there with me at all.

Hi, I said. I wanted to tell her about Ryan saying sorry and about how maybe it was OK and we didn't need to do anything. We only had a year to go and then we'd be done and that it wasn't so long, that when we left we wouldn't even remember what had happened.

Are you ready? she said. I want to get there before they do.

The words were jammed up, just below my throat, like logs blocking a river. They were words but they were also hesitations and repetitions and pauses and stammers and gaps and mistakes.

She had already started away. I followed her.

7

We leave the buildings behind and trudge across the field. The grass is roiled to mud, the running track nearly entirely obscured. The cricket nets are torn and tangled with loose branches, the catch of balls buried in the far corners, someone's abandoned shirt. Looking back the school buildings are lost to the deluge, the occasional glow of a window. The storm is coming down, blurring my vision. The sound of the wind is nearly hidden by the downpour but at moments it emerges. It is bending me nearly double, threatening to stop us making it altogether. Now and then September walks beside me, holding my hand, tapping her excitement onto my wrist with her fingers; now and then she forges ahead, not looking back, hands buried in her pockets. I hurry to keep up, the smell of the rotting grass, my damp hair. At the end of the field there are trees and the undergrowth is thick, clumps of nettles, tall grass.

*

In the Settle House I am saying something, the words twisting my jaw. And through the trees – through the trees –

And through the trees as we walk I see flashes of September, kicking at the muddy ground and the trunks, her face turned up to the sky. It's been a long time since I came to this part of the school. The ground grows rough and the roots of trees churn upwards. The rain drops fall inside the neck of my waterproof and wet the collar of my dress, dribble off the end of my nose. September is already a good way into the trees, moving doggedly forward, obscured by the trunks; in sight again. It is almost as if she has forgotten I am here at all. She is not here for me, I think, and pause, consider going back to the school, hiding in the toilet until it is over or ringing Mum and saying, loud, down the phone: I don't want to do it. I'm frightened. I don't know what to do.

I hesitate, on the border of the tree line. Miserable beneath the weight of the wind, trying to breathe. Peering to make out the cage of the old tennis courts, just being able to see the broken beam of the floodlight or the squat body of the shed. Raising my hands to cup my mouth, thinking maybe to call September; my hands dropping to my side, my voice falling away.

Once I have decided to go on, I rush to keep up and nearly trip and go down, the nettles in some places almost as high as my head. The forest rumbles around us and I look up at the sky through the trees and it is white and there is the distant noise of something that might be thunder or cars passing on the new main road. I can see the tennis court clearly now and the shed, which September is moving towards. The shed is squat and moss-roofed, one of the walls at an awkward, slumped angle, another rotting away so that it is possible to see inside. I hold on to the trunks of trees and push myself forward, only pausing to look back to see if Lily or any of the others have come yet but the school field is big and empty and the trees cluster close. There is a low whistling sound in my ears, a frequency perhaps only I can hear.

In the Settle House my body is disconnecting from itself, losing shape and form, tangling with memory.

I come to the shed; there is the smell of the garlic that grows along the riverbank. September is inside, kicking at the loose walls, wide-eyed, jigging from foot to foot and I try to reach out and touch her, hold on to her. What would I say to her if I managed to still her for a moment? The shed is strewn with decaying wooden rackets, the walls softening beneath the pressure of growing weeds. I reach out for her. I will say something to distract her, a question, I will ask her if she remembers – or I will grab her by the shoulders and shake her until this plan falls out.

I will grab her by the shoulders and shake her until what happened here falls right out of her and right out of me.

But she is – bobbing out of reach, stepping back out of the shed and into the rain, flashing a languid smile towards me. She is moving towards the swampy tennis court. I hold on to the door and watch her. I want to go out, follow her towards the courts which are swimming with water, one of the big, rusting floodlights has switched on and is glowing eerily through the dank air. I want to stay in the shed, crouch down, wait until it is over. From a little way off I think I hear a voice shouting, Lily and the others perhaps, on their way towards us. September is picking her way through the undergrowth, one hand running along the mesh fence, moving towards the entrance to the court. In my chest I feel a shout rising, almost there, filling my mouth like wine. She comes into the tennis court and kicks at the deep water, throwing it upwards so that it seems to hang frozen for a moment in the fizzing beam from the floodlight and then fall back. There is a noise like wood breaking and I look up.

The rain is pelting down and the trees are swaying, beaten, around us and above – above there is the shudder of imminent movement. One of the trees on the far side of the court, just beside the fence, is shifting, its roots emerging from the earth as if it might walk away from that place. September is laughing and laughing, her blonde head tipped back, her mouth open. I shout her name, September, watch out. She turns towards me. The tree – falls silently, sideways, and into the largest of the floodlights which is heaved unceremoniously from the ground, the squeal of loosening metal, the tree's trailing, dying body bringing the floodlight crashing down through the old fence into the water on the court which for a moment is illuminated, charged with – light. There is the smell of dampened fire, smoke. Someone is shouting. September's body bent backwards by some force that only later I will know is electricity. And I am trying to run forward but the shed is buckling around me, the walls caving in and I am trapped and someone is shouting and shouting and it is – someone is shouting – and it is me.

PART THREE

Sheela

There was, first, the phone call from the school. The voice of the receptionist, which she recognised, the too-long pause, the hitch of nasal breath. Instantly she had thought: it's July. Something has happened to her (and yes, it was possible she had thought: September has done something to her). Except it wasn't July after all.

The drive over. Dangerous in the storm, swerving in and out of the rain-hidden lane, driving through red lights she had only just seen in the gloom, the hurtling cars coming at her out of nothing and only just missing. What had she thought about then, hands gripping the wheel, yelling at passing motorists? She had thought of the girl's father. Of the Copenhagen summer when she'd first met him, a man in a bar who had come over to the table where she was sitting with a friend and spoken to her in a language she did not understand. How later, in perfect English, he'd said: I'd like to show you the city. And later, in perfect English, he'd said: I'd like us to move in together. Cavalierly swooping her bags out of reach, opening doors, tapping her lips to stop her from speaking.

She was nearly there now, cutting the last corner so she heard the wing mirror smashing. Thinking of September. Firstborn, crackling lightning-haired child, his eyes, the inflection of his voice inside her soft mouth, his determination and avarice; as if he had not died but somehow seeped into the skin of the child. It was not fair to think such things. The car mounting the kerb and then thumping down, her teeth closing over her tongue. Her firstborn, running rampage, bloody-nosed child, July tugged behind like a kite. Sometimes to look at her the fear was so large she felt like it might lift her by her shoulders and carry her away.

September was her father's daughter. A darkening of worry at the threshold of their good life.

The way the door handle used to turn in the dark, in the night, in whichever house they had hidden in. The image of his body in that swimming pool, pruned, open-eyed. Even then sitting up to watch the door and the windows, thinking: even dead, even dead, even dead.

The school was lit by the green and blue lights from an ambulance. From the car she could hear the sound of the stretcher bumping down the steps. Perhaps it was a joke September was playing, a prank taken – as ever – too far. How many children do you have? One. Why did you decide to have one child? I didn't, I didn't, I didn't. July's face through the open back doors of the ambulance, the blanket that smelled of antiseptic wrapped around her shoulders, her roving eyes landing on Sheela's face and pinning to it in a way they never had before.

When Sheela's mother died there had been bank accounts to close, a house in India to sell, books and kitchen implements to sort through. But daughters leave so little behind. It seemed so September-like not to leave her debris to focus on, to fill the days with. There was her bedroom – also July's – which was neat and tidy; a book on the sofa she thought September might have been reading, a half-eaten yogurt in the fridge which might or might not have belonged to her. In the attic there were boxes of report cards, drawings she had done as a child where all the fish were coloured in brown and black. There were clothes in the laundry basket and a pair of tweezers in the medicine cabinet. Sheela put everything she could find on the bed and lay down among these forgotten, left-behind objects. If she waited for enough time September would come back to find them, padding muddy-footed through the silent house, climbing up onto the bed to lie beside her. The pain was different from the way she'd felt when her mother died or with Peter. It had been possible then to compartmentalise, however ineptly, the grief, to whittle it down into smaller sections. Losing September was not like that. There was no moment when she did not remember what had happened and feel the pressure of that remembering up and down her arms, curled in her stomach, knotted in her hair, digging like nodules into her skin. She lay on the bed and waited for her to come back but she could not lie there forever. She had another daughter.

July's presence pulled Sheela from her bed in Oxford, forced clothes onto her body. She brushed her teeth; she still had one daughter left. Except July was sitting at the kitchen table wearing September's dress, talking in September's voice, looking up at her with September's suspicious gaze. July had always looked like her daughter in a way that September didn't. She would see people's eyes on the street swivelling to her fairer daughter and know they were wondering if she'd kidnapped her. When someone died they didn't live on inside us, they were just gone. She made July food and brushed her hair out and tried to explain to her what had happened but July didn't seem to hear her. But then who was she to persuade someone else? Still, every time she heard a noise in the house she thought it was September, every time someone was at the door or on the phone she was prepared to see her, hear her voice. *Only joking, that was a good one, wasn't it?*

This was the step where September had sat when she was naughty, scowling. This was the wall where Sheela had recorded their heights, September always a little taller. This was the door September had slammed once and then, for good measure she said later, again. This was the hole she had made with a broken chair leg and yes, she had been in serious trouble for that one. This was the glass she'd liked best and never let anyone else drink from. July was talking to herself in her bedroom. This was the place where / this was the moment when / this was the wall the floor the seat the table.

Small memories coming back. The time she fell into the rose bushes and lay grim-jawed and damp-cheeked on the sofa while Sheela picked out the thorns. The way September had jigged inside her, never still, especially at night, the shocked wave of that first contraction coming in the early morning as Sheela had bent forward to reach for the milk. The argument about the tooth fairy, September's face, her fingers closed around the tooth, refusing to let it go.

When that first contraction came she clenched her eyes shut and wished it away. Peter was listening to the radio in the bedroom. They had been in the Settle House for a month. It had been just over three years since she'd met him and already it was bad. She used to go into the bathroom and lock the door for hours, wait to see if he would leave. He'd gone out for the day and September had emerged into the house from inside her, the sheets softened with blood, the afterbirth thrown into the corner, the tiny body quivering, releasing and then clenching her finger. The house had seemed different that day. She'd never liked it much but she liked it then, the way she and it waited together for the small, new thing to come into the world, the way the walls contracted around her first, glorious cry. There were memories of September in the Settle House but they seemed nearly painless in a way they weren't in Oxford; it would be better there. If she could grieve her anywhere it was there.

Peter buried like a broken bottle inside her child. Her child who was capable of manipulation and cruelty and who sometimes treated her sister like she was a receptacle, carried around, picked up and then put back down, everything poured into her.

When Sheela was still young she would steal coins from her mother's purse and dig them into the soft flesh of her arms or stomach, grinding in. The lurking trepidation of dreams would inhabit the day and she would wonder how anyone stood it, all the walking and talking, all the pretending. The pills the doctors put her on made her slow-minded. They drove her through her teenage years in a sort of stupor, losing hours. Off the pills the distance from her to the sadness had lengthened but it was still there, lingering, murky with heat haze. With Peter she had felt it drawing near again, throwing the days off-kilter, impossible to think she would ever feel good once more. And now, yes, here it was. Old familiar body docking into that well-worn station. The blue dread coming in, getting right inside her through her mouth and ears, through her skin. Worse than it had ever been. Of course.

Her first child was dead.

The bed in the Settle House stank but she dragged herself into it and pulled the duvet over her head and the despair came in like a seething cloud of insects and lost her. She couldn't tell where she ended and the house began. Nor where the house ended and she began.

Up in the night. Making chilli in the kitchen for July, cooking in the darkness; exhausted after chopping a single onion, grinding the knife down onto the bulbs of garlic and finding herself undone by it. Behind her in the sitting room the sofa made a sound as if someone had just sat down. She took a spoonful of chilli and tried to imagine what it would feel like to care about having a body again. She kept thinking she heard September's voice calling. She kept thinking that Peter was there, just out of view, waiting for her to sleep. He would always be there when the sadness came back down, bringing him with it. Dead had never been dead.

She got up and drew pictures of the Settle House and September moving around the rooms. The bed held her in place or she held it in place.

September had come easily, quickly, but July had been an emergency Caesarean because of the position in which she'd been lying, sideways, arms curled protectively around her head. The strangeness of it, so different from the seizing pain of September. The hospital room had been filled with people, indistinguishable behind their masks. One of them should have been Peter but he wasn't there again. She wasn't sure where he was. A screen was positioned, cutting her in half. She wished she could see what they were doing, know when to expect to hold the baby. There was the feeling of hands riffling inside her, an overwhelming pressure that came and went. Then the baby was out and on her chest, its skin covered in a soft, stinking cream, its eyes wide and alert.

In the years when the girls were young she had wanted to write about what it was like to house things inside her, how it was possible to be both skin and flesh and also mortar and plaster. She pitied the Settle House and the house in Oxford then, understood better what it felt like to be filled up with noise and pain, understood why the walls sometimes seemed to crumple in on themselves. After she'd given birth she felt emptied out, like a beloved house closed up for the winter.

For such a long time the sense that her body did not belong to her continued. It had been that way in the later days with the girls' father and she felt it again with them inside her, swelling her, unstoppable, using her body as a resting stop. Later, in the Settle House, she imagined the book she would write, the pictures she would draw in which a woman with dark hair would watch her skin turning dense and crumbly, feel her legs turn brick and her arms to chimneys. She had never written it and perhaps, now, she never would. She wasn't sure if she would ever really write again.

Or would she write about that dead daughter? It was inconceivable in this moment but perhaps she would. For nearly seventeen years two threads had emerged from her body and gone out into the world, connecting her to them. It did not feel, now, as if one of the threads was cut, only that it went to a place where she could not follow. Fucking shitting hell she wanted to go into a supermarket and break every glass thing she could find. She wanted to bring on the end of the world and if it was possible she would find the beginning of time and draw it back, the consequences be damned, and back until that dead daughter re-emerged into the house in Oxford where their happiness had been tenuous but, always, there. She would give her pound of flesh if it was necessary, just to know there was no longer an absence where there had once been furious, ridiculous presence.

She has dreams of those early, child-filled days. She sees warnings where there had been none, thinks over and over: why hadn't I stopped it? Did it mean something that September always threw her food on the floor as a toddler? Did it mean something that she used to tug out Sheela's hair when she was breastfeeding? Did it mean something that she had not cried on the first day of nursery like the other children, only walked, without looking back, into the school? Did it mean something that her father was a man whose hate so closely resembled his love?

July

1

It is not entirely clear how much time has passed.

I get the milk out of the fridge and drink straight from the bottle, spilling it down my front, the sound of it pattering onto the floor.

She is dead.

Except it is not possible to kill September.

I look for her in the bathroom mirror. I can see her, moving fast, looking out at me with her loving, awful face. I can see her. I look over my shoulder, try and catch her out. GOT YOU. She isn't there. Mirror September loses her shit.

Memories come back to me from wherever they were hidden in the garden of my insides: being alone for months and months and months. Sleeping without her in a cold bed and being so mad that I thought she was there. Speaking in her voice on the beach and in the house and in the car. Playing September Says by myself. Eating food by myself. Speaking to myself.

The sink catches me on the way down, the floor holds me up. She is dead. She is not dead. She is dead. She is not dead.

I put my cheek against the floor. Yes. Of course. She is dead. There is something flapping in my chest, like the bird that I had seen force its way out from the wall, its wings shuttering open and closed. I am not a person without her. My sister is a black hole my sister is a falling tree my sister is the sea.

It is better to be mad than this. It is better to be mad.

I get it together for a moment. I go into the other room, sit on the sofa and look at John on the floor. He looks very young, his red hair and freckled skin, his mouth open as he sleeps. I remember, as if it is just happening, being on the beach and knowing that I wanted him and that he wanted me too. September hadn't been there but somehow I'd been speaking like her, with her confidence and lack of care. I'd lifted my dress over my head and gone into the sea, how cold it had been, the burn of the salt, John's tongue and mine, the gritty sand on the back of my legs, the lift and drop of pain, the stammer of our chests together.

*

I try and move but nothing that once belonged to me will do what it is told. If September were here she would say … if September were here she would laugh … if September were here she wouldn't allow any of … I go back into the bathroom and stand over the toilet because I might be sick and I wait for her to hold my hair back but she doesn't. And she doesn't and she doesn't and she doesn't and she never will again.

I am in bed. I go downstairs. John is gone, the door not quite caught closed. There has never been anyone but September. There has barely even been me. I jam my fingers into my mouth and bite down on my knuckles. I scratch at my arm, baring my teeth at the good-bad feeling of it. The mark has jumped in size again, is wrapping around my shoulder now, tendrils of it across my chest, curling up towards my face.

Where to go from this place? September says: buck up, July-bug. September says: stop moping around. September says: jump off a cliff if you're going to be so grumpy. I go to the wall and dig my fingers into the plaster and say: take me instead. Take me.

The light in the house changes. My mind moves from one conclusion to another. I understand that September is dead and had never been there at all. That the thoughts I had been certain were hers were mine all along. The events of the last few days clarify. My head feels full of hollows. I have never seen myself without her also there, her body pushing mine out of the frame. When I look from the corner of my eye I think I see something moving, not out in the room but somehow inside me, crawling beneath the surface. I will hold on. A decision that is not a decision lingers and then is made. I will keep her here.

All the bad things September did. Made me promise with blood. Made me have the same birthday as her. Broke my bike. Was horrid to Mum. Made me horrid to Mum. Made me steal the perfume. Tripped me up. Held me under the water. Shaved off one of my eyebrows. Too many other things to fit on a list.

All the good things September did. Loved me. Looked after me. Was me.

2

I get caught up in a daydream where September is alive and we are the characters from our favourite TV series. September is Hadley, with blue rubber gloves in her pocket and a photographic memory. I am Bell, with a monocle and a stutter. We are in Oxford, in the tunnels that run between colleges, and Hadley has drowned in an ancient crypt we uncover. For a time I am alone, trying and failing to solve crimes, but then I work out a way to bring her back by removing one of my own ribs and using an ancient Egyptian technique I find in a very old book in the Bodleian Library. For a time Hadley is odd, death-lingering, speaks with a lisp and uses sentences that don't sound like her. Eventually, though, she gets better and we find what we have been looking for. Buried beneath the Oxford streets, in the cellars and tunnels and hidden corners: the answer we have been searching for.

*

It is dark outside. I go from room to room and turn on all the lights. I have a headache, a bad one, radiating from my temples and around my head like a band. I lie on the sofa and close my eyes to see if it will go away but it only gets worse. I think of going upstairs to find Mum and tell her what has happened, that I thought September was alive but now I know she is dead, but there is a heaviness on my shoulders and chest and I cannot move. My skin itches and I am almost certain I can feel the mark carry on spreading, gouging out the fresh skin and laying down a new, gutted track.

Is it better that she is dead? I put my fingernails into the skin close to my eyes. I pull my hair and white starlings explode behind my lids. I gnaw my lip until it bursts. I scratch at my thighs. Is it better that she is dead?

The Settle House has roots in the earth. When she was ten years old September told Mum that we would have one birthday between the two of us. Sometimes I feel words slipping in my mind, loose as milk teeth, ready for her to speak hers in their place. September had stabbed the tyres on my bike with a screwdriver and we rode her bike together, through the university parks and up the wrong side of the road, past the Pitt Rivers, screaming like hyena at people on the pavements. If words are milk teeth then September is the box they are kept in. She says: listen to me, July. She says: don't worry, July.

*

I realise that my hands are moving but that I cannot feel them. I try to open and close my fingers but they don't respond. My arms are numb from the elbow down. My tongue feels like a lump of bread in my mouth, my toes begin to lose all feeling. The band of the headache squeezes and squeezes, unbearable, and then suddenly, releases.

I think of all the things I can do now she is gone. Eat what I like, sleep, talk to Mum, go for walks, watch what I want, make friends with some of the people on the beach, make friends with anyone I like. It is freedom.

No. No. No. No. No. No. No. No. No. No.

Yes.

September says hold your breath. Hold it forever. Hold it for sixteen years. September says get into the grate so I can build a fire from you. September says here's a knife, cut a hole in your belly so I can live inside you.

Go to whichever university I want to go to. Live in whatever city I want to live in. Watch what I want to watch on the television. Eat chocolate and apples and red peppers and Marmite and mincemeat.

3

We are eleven years old and we are waiting to see the eclipse. We've watched them on YouTube and read about them on Wikipedia. An eclipse is the obscuring of light from one celestial body by the passage of another. We are in the spare room in the house in Oxford and it is hot and stuffy, the rafters clogged with spiderwebs. Mum is working in her study and does not know we are here. No one knows we are here. September is holding the box cutter like a weapon, she has already sliced half a hole in the cardboard cereal packet we have taken from the kitchen.

You do the rest?

I shake my head. She is holding out the box cutter, the blade extended from the scratched plastic casing.

Come on. Otherwise it doesn't belong to both of us.

I take the cutter from her. I know from experience that she won't back down. One of the houses opposite is chopping down the big oak in the front garden and there is the noise of the whirring blades, the air outside clogged with sawdust. I lay the cardboard onto the scrap wood we'd found in Mum's study and push the blade down. The pressure is off, or my hand is shaking, and the blade goes through the cardboard and then out sharply, slicing smoothly and without much pain into my thumb. I look at the broken skin until the blood starts to come. I can feel myself starting to soften, my knees bending.

Don't worry, September says. She takes the box cutter from me, wedges it firmly down into the soft pad of her own thumb until blood wells up around the blade. See, she says, nothing to worry about. She laughs at me and then grows still.

I know then that something is coming. The blood from her thumb has smeared across her hands and is on the pinhole projector, darker on the cardboard. She rubs her thumb against each cheek and leaves smears of a war wound behind, gestures for me to do the same but I am frozen. She grabs for the box cutter and holds it up so that the thin metal blade is against her throat. I can see the skin puckering.

If I died, would you? she says.

It is not the first time she has asked such a thing. *If I was kidnapped would you offer yourself in my place? If a double was here would you know it wasn't me? If I lost a limb would you cut off one of yours?* There is only ever, of course, one answer.

Yes, I say. I know I would.

I expect her to put the box cutter down but she doesn't move, her eyes very pale, not dissimilar to the eyes of the cats that glow from the end of the garden.

If one of us was going to die and we could choose which it would be, would you die for me? she says.

I can feel my tongue fumbling.

Yes, of course. It would be me.

You promise?

Yes. Yes.

Write it down. She puts the box cutter away and I feel relieved, at least, at that. I would have said anything, done anything.

There is a bag of old sketch pads belonging to Mum, the pages crowded with our faces. September searches until she finds a pencil and hands it to me, opens one of the sketch pads to an empty page.

Write it down. If you write it down you won't ever break it.

I hold the pencil and then squat down and write: If there could be only one of us it would be you.

September tears the paper free and puts it in her pocket and then holds me, the smell of her all around.

4

I go to the bottom of the stairs thinking I will climb up, go find Mum and tell her that I understand what has happened. But with a foot on the first step I pause. A change in the air or in the blood. There is September's smell all around me the way there had been that day, muffling me. The stairs ahead are blurred, I cannot make out the separate steps. I think about everything that is coming, everything that will happen. My foot shakes. It is awful, all of this possibility. It is awful to have anything other than grief but I think about finishing school and perhaps going to university and then, after, getting a job I like or travelling and meeting someone and maybe living with them. I think about having sex again, better this time and maybe learning to cook or reading a book she didn't want to read. And buried between each word, each possible outcome, is this: I'll let you go. I won't keep you. I'll live.

*

I carry on up the stairs and along the corridor and open the door to Mum's room. The duvet is thick and her body is warm with sleep. I lie against her and she says, What is it, July? What is it?

There is the smell of her and, beneath, of September, too.

What is it? She holds her cheek to the side of my cheek in a way I remember her doing but that hasn't happened for a long time. I can see September in her, in the shape of her nose and mouth, in the way – even – that she blinks. I do not know how to tell her everything that I need to say. I do not know where the beginning is. It is buried back at that tennis court, in the debris from the collapsed shed, in the ambulance with the discarded syringes and stained sheets. I do not know how to tell her that I have been living with the ghost of September strung around my neck.

She's dead, I say.

Grief is a house with no windows or doors and no way of telling the time. Sleeping curled against Mum's back, arm thrown over her so that – in the night, in the dark – her shoulders and hair in my mouth could belong to anyone. Could belong to September. Everything shutting down, all the lights turning off inside, not needing to eat or go to the bathroom or even really sleep although that's all I seemed to do, the smell of myself beneath the blanket, the click of the house turning over like an idling car. Waking one night and not knowing why. Turning over and feeling the sodden pyjama bottoms against my legs, the smell of my own urine, the sheet beneath me soaked. The spike of a headache in the centre of my forehead, drilling right down. The moonlight from the bare window catching the water in the bucket Mum brings up, the rasp of the sponge on my legs and arms. The sheet tugged off the bed, balled up, the stink of ammonia. Her hands dropping the sponge in, wringing it out, lifting my hair, laying the warmth against the back of my neck.

We liked cheese and onion sandwiches. We liked a programme called *33* and David Attenborough. We liked the sea. We liked long car journeys. We liked reading the twist in books first. We liked beans on toast. We liked stolen wine. We liked long baths. We liked *Desert Island Discs*. We liked lie-ins. We liked the last biscuit in the packet. We liked campfires. We liked sofas. We liked tents in the sitting room. We liked things we found in the garden. We liked the Internet. We liked white dresses with black tights. We liked stolen perfume. We liked birthdays. We liked cake. We liked bare legs. We liked promises. We liked a song called 'What's your name?' We liked the salt at the bottom of the crisp packet. We liked wearing one scarf at the same time. We liked not having a dad. We liked not having friends. We liked the rain. We liked the school field.

One morning Mum says I can't have sandwiches in bed any more and we fight.

You don't understand, I say. You can't possibly understand. Leave me alone.

She pulls the duvet off and onto the floor, lets it pool around her legs. I do understand. But we have to get up. You're going to waste away. She tugs the curtains open so the light falls onto the bed, hurts my eyes. September wouldn't want this.

You don't know anything, I think but I don't say it. She goes to make tea. I count the days; it has been nearly a week since I understood that she was dead. I have a headache that seems to start in my gums and then radiate upwards. Mum calls for me from downstairs. In a moment it is possible to forget and then remember all over again.

We sit on the sofa and eat sandwiches, slurp at too-hot tea. It is polite, like a dinner party; I do not know how to talk to her without September between us like a bridge and a wall all at the same time.

Do you feel like you've been in space and only just come down? I say.

Sure, she says, yes. All the time.

Like you've been eating space food and using a space toilet and your arms and legs aren't used to gravity?

Yes.

We watch YouTube videos of women astronauts washing their hair in space. Mum cackles at the water bubbles which get loose and float off, a laugh so like September's I find myself looking around for her, expectant, excited to see her. Mum says she wants to go for a walk but the thought of leaving the house makes me shaky so we stay on the sofa, curled up the way September and I would be. I think about telling her that though I have never been sadder when I found out September was dead, part of me was relieved. I don't think I can say such a thing. She puts some frozen pizzas in the oven for dinner, crouching down to check the temperature.

One day we drive to Homebase and buy: paint, picture frames, a new double bed to replace the bunk beds, a fern, a succulent, two cacti, lamps, a small table, a table-cloth, mugs with S and J on them, wine glasses, a vase, picture hooks, a coffee maker, bath sealant and bleach. We repaint the house and put up pictures and move the furniture around.

One day I do not think of September for ten minutes. One day I think again about what it would be like if September were still alive and I do not know which is worse.

One day I get accepted to a university I have applied to. Not the first one on my list but not the last either. Mum puts on the radio and we pack almost everything I own into boxes. Her handwriting is nearly illegible. She writes: COOKRY, BKS, BD SHEETS, CLOTHES. Everything fits in the back seat of the car. We stop at a service station and eat pasta salad and carrot cake. We talk about what September would have done at university, whether we would have gone to the same place. We would. We get stuck in the complicated one-way system in the city and Mum has a shouting argument with another driver while I load all my stuff out of the car onto the pavement.

One day I think: this is not the way I would have done this if she were here. I am taking a shortcut through a park and the thought comes to me and lies down on my shoulders. I want to sit on a bench but my legs won't do what I tell them, I walk fast out of the park and along the busy road, car exhaust, the sound of phones going off, everyone walking in one direction or the other. The thought expands. Here it is. Here is the truth. This is not the way I would have done this if she were here. I would not have been able to live if she were here.

5

This is not what happened.
  This
  is
  not
  what
  happened.

The Settle House gawps around me. My foot is lifted up onto the first step of the stairs. My right hand is closed around the banister. I try to move my other foot up onto the step but something stops me. My mouth is very dry, as if I have been standing here for a long time. I can feel the tears gathering just before dropping. I promised, I think, I haven't forgotten. But the thought is tangled, not quite mine. There is something lingering behind the words, just out of sight, a shifting. I promised and the words grow, fill in, turn solid and thick. I think: I love you I love you I love you and feel my jaw opening without my say-so, the words forced out into the space in front of me. IloveyouIloveyouIloveyouIloveyou.

And then I feel, like a chilly exhalation, September arriving into me. She does not come gently or with peaceful intentions. My sister is a black hole my sister is a bricked-up window my sister is a house on fire my sister is a car crash my sister is a long night my sister is a battle my sister is here. September is holding my lips shut. I understand, for the first time, the promise that I made her and exactly what it means: If there could be only one of us it would be you. My arms are yours, my legs are yours, my heart and lungs and stomach and fingers and eyes are yours. She is familiar as a song, my hands lifting without my say-so, my legs clicking to attention. A moment where I think no (nononononon-onono) but it is too late. There is someone else inside me, using my mouth to speak, holding me still.

6

If brains are houses with many rooms then I live in the basement. It is dark and quiet. Sometimes there is the noise of movement overhead, as of water passing through pipes or something slowly digested. At times there is a bright light and the place I live in is revealed. All corners and under-stair compartments, small gaps. The walls are wet to the touch. I have grown small to fit, elongated like the adders that breed in the long grass by the beach.

If brains are houses with many rooms then September lives in every single one. The rooms are big as churches and she swells and balloons to fit them, her thoughts loud as foghorns and ringing through the rooms like bells. I do not know what September's rooms looks like but when I imagine them they are the beach, low tide, miles of sand, endless water. Sometimes I think about the ant farm and I understand that is what it is like in here, everything crushing down, all the tunnels collapsing moments after I have crawled out of them.

One Sunday morning I bake a cake, take a slice with a cup of tea out into the garden. It is sunny and there is the smell of the sea and of the rosemary that has grown and grown. Earlier, I'd looked in the mirror and there was white in my hair and I barely recognised my face. I'd called for Mum but the house was empty. I tried to count the years, work out what I had missed, but the knowledge was too much and I let it go. In the sunny garden I can feel September inside me, a small insistence, a reminder. I hold my hands on the table and look at them and think how, really, they had never belonged to me. I remember the way September moved through the storm that killed her, dancing between the tree trunks, laughing at the sky. She was alive, she was so alive then that she stole living from those around her. I was in the background of the memory, barely there, a slip of colour, a shadow. And before, when we were young, there had never really been anyone but September. I was an appendage. I was September's sister.

My thoughts feel blurred, unclear. September is starting to shift inside me. I close my eyes. It was always supposed to be this way. It could never have been any way but this. It should have been me that day. I can hear September murmuring now, rising up. I had promised a long time ago. Promised what? Promised everything. Here it is. I lay it out now. Here is everything I have.

Acknowledgements

Thanks are due to too many people to fit on a page. Any mistakes in this book are my own. Any successes could not have been achieved without the following:

Sarah McGrath at Riverhead. Thank you for giving not just this but the next book a chance. To every publisher who has taken this book on.

Chris Wellbelove my agent who works on every word I write with patience and humour, to whom this book belongs almost as much as to me.

Everyone at Aitken Alexander. Lesley, Anna, Lisa, Alex, Clare, Amy, Monica.

My editor Ana Fletcher who I cannot imagine writing without. Who always succeeds in lifting an idea from the mess, dusting it off, bringing it to light.

Mia, Joe, Suzanne, Daisy, Michal. Jonathan Cape and all who sail in her.

Tom, Kiran and Sarvat for continuing to be the people to go to both in writing and in life.

Jess, Lucy, Jessie, Gabby, Paul, Joseph Nick, Laura, Ric, Matt, Ellie, Amelie, Ruby.

Susie, Martin and Anna Bradshaw for making me part of the family.

My grandfather.

My grandmother for her bravery and fierceness.

Polly and Jake.

My dad for his steadfastness, for his love, for his cooking. For always being there.

My mum for watching horror films she doesn't really want to watch with me. For reading every book I give her. For always being there.

Matt, for agreeing to take on the books as well as the person. For everything you have done and continue to do. To all that is ahead of us.

To the booksellers.

To you, whoever you are, for giving this book a chance.